TRIANGLE PUBLISHING

LOST
IN
EDEN

I0664567

VOLUME ONE

Published by Triangle Publishing LLC
© 2015

ISBN: 0692382372
First Edition

Email address: bigstriggs@yahoo.com

David Greenway @ Greenway Studios: Cover Design
Donald Payne: Format
Anthony Striggles: Editor

Table of Contents

Preacha' Man : Algie Striggles 1

Family Affairs : Anthony Striggles...32

Judgment Day : Rebecca Striggles...78

The Pleasure of Sin : Arie Olah 112

Lost In Eden : Anthony Striggles 128

Preacha' Man

Written By: Algie Striggles

SUNDAY SERVICE

-CHAPTER 1-

Reverend Elias Davidson had preached a very fiery soul-stirring sermon that morning. He felt tired as if he had just worked-out at the health spa. Nevertheless, he stood in the doorway and greeted all of his parishioners as they left the sanctuary.

As the members filed out of the church they all told him how his message affected them. He received handshakes from the men, and hugs from most of the women. There were several attractive women in this congregation, some of whom he had bedded. Some women even joined the church because they were sexually attracted to Rev. Davidson. He was fifty-two and many say he resembled Clifton Davis, the actor. God also *endowed* him with a *big blessing* in the manhood department.

When it was their turn to greet this *Man of God* many of the women would hug him, pressing their pelvises into him. Some would just inhale his scent, while others whispered dirty secrets in his ear. One sister was brazen enough to quickly stick her tongue in his ear.

All the attention caused Rev. Davidson's dick to stand erect like a church steeple. He looked over at his wife, who was seated in a

1

pew patiently waiting for him, and wondered why she couldn't light his fire anymore. There was a time when he couldn't keep his hands off and his dick out of her. That time seemed so long ago.

"Elias what's the matter?" asked Delores, his wife.

This snapped him out of his daydream.

"Nothing, I was just thinking about something," replied Rev. Davidson.

"Are you ready to leave?" she asked.

"Not yet. I still have some things to do before going home."

"Well, I'll have dinner ready when you get there." She turned to go find their seventeen-year-old daughter Alexis, and their fifteen year old son Mario.

Delores was fifty, and not hard on the eyes. To the Rev.'s dismay, she felt as if she had to look a certain way being a pastor's wife. She didn't wear anything revealing or clingy. Alexis, who was already a dime-piece, often ridiculed her mother by telling her she dressed like the Amish. That was not the woman that Elias fell in *lust* with at first sight. Before her spiritual transformation, she was vibrant with what seemed like an insatiable appetite for sex. Sometimes all she had to do was look at Elias and his dick would stiffen. Then all of a sudden she changed. The problem with that was Elias didn't; his appetite for sex and for sexy women did not diminish. As the old saying goes, *what you did to get him, you've got to do to keep him.* Well, it was apparent that Delores did not receive that memo; which caused Elias to have to find other outlets for his sexual urges.

2

After just about everyone had left, the Rev. and his head deacon went into the office to tally up the day's offering. That was something Deacon Ellis loved to do, because he always got a nice cut of the pot.

"Got damn!" You preached so hard I thought dem muh' fuckas was gonna start throwin' they checkbooks, wallets, purses, bridge-cards, and panties at you," spat the crooked deacon.

Rev. Elias Davidson just laughed and said, "Hell, I was preachin' so good *my* dick got hard."

These supposed men of God talked like they were down at their favorite bar or something. As the deacon put the remainder of the money, that wasn't in their pockets, in a bank bag, there was a knock at the door.

Before either man could respond, the door to the office opened. In walked Theresa Washington one of the sexiest women to walk this here earth. Her face wasn't anything to sing about, but her persona oozed sensuality. She was thirty-five, with the body of a stripper. She could make a nigga almost bust a nut on himself just by strolling past him. Men worshiped her. Women hated and envied her; because they knew the pussy power she possessed could cause their men to leave them. Theresa was the church secretary. The *high and holy* women of the church wanted to crucify her.

Deacon Ellis cleared his throat, and adjusted his pants to accommodate his growing erection.

"Well I guess my work here is done," said the deacon. He winked at the Rev and gave him a knowing nod of the head.

"Grace and Peace!" exclaimed Theresa.

He looked at her like *hoe whatever*; but said, "Praise the Lord," as he headed out the door.

As Theresa closed the door Rev. Davidson asked her who she thought she was fooling with that fake ass church shit.

"I got that bitch Delores fooled. Don't I?"

"Watch what you say about her. She's still my wife and the mother of my kids."

"Well enough talkin' about her; and enough talkin' period. I want to use my mouth and tongue for something else right now," Theresa freakily replied.

Hearing this, Rev David started stroking his dick through his pants, and licking his lips.

He said, "Enough talkin' then. Take me to heaven."

Theresa walked up to him, and they molested each other's mouths with their tongues. He took his hands and grabbed both of her fat and juicy ass cheeks through her dress. She was wearing a lace thong. She groaned, and was already wet in her panties. She took one hand from around the back of his neck and groped his throbbing penis.

Pre-cum started to ooze out of his mushroom shaped dickhead. As she started undoing his belt and pants, he started undoing the zipper on the back of her dress. They stopped tonsil fucking long enough for her to let her dress drop to the floor.

4

"Got damn," was all Rev. Davidson could manage to say.

While he stroked his member, Theresa got on her knees and started licking the good Rev.'s balls. She then placed both of them in her mouth and began humming.

"Ooh shit," was all Rev. Davidson could utter while his eyes rolled up in his head.

Theresa took her tongue and licked the pre-cum out of the mouth of his dick. She then started vigorously sucking on his rock-hard 9 inches. With very little effort or gagging she swallowed him whole. By then, the Rev. had a handful of her hair, as if he was holding on for dear life. Her head game was so good he had already begun building up an explosive climax.

He didn't want to cum yet; so he took her face in his hands and throatily said, "My turn."

Theresa got off the floor and grabbed both of her breasts.

"You like this?" she asked as she flicked her erect nipples with her tongue.

"Hell yeah," said the Rev. "Let me do that for you though."
He then grabbed her flawless, perky tits and sucked on her nipples like a hungry infant. This elicited moans of pleasure from Theresa. After scooping her up in his arms, he carried her over to the couch. He laid her down and kissed from her toes up to her inner thighs. He stopped right before he got to the *Promised Land*.

There was no hair on her pussy; which is how the Rev. told her he liked it. With his thumb, he manipulated her clitoris. He then dove in face first like he was bobbing for apples. He licked, sucked, and nibbled so much that he broke into a sweat. In his mind he was *doing the damn thang*. All Theresa could think was *thank God he has a big dick, 'cause he sho' can't eat no pussy*. She patronized him; however, making so much noise you would think she was having multiple orgasms.

After a few minutes of this she said, "Fuck me big daddy".

"How bad do you want this dick?" asked the Rev. as he teasingly stroked it.

"Like the song says 'I ain't too proud to beg,'" said Theresa.

Marwan pulled up to his parents' house in his new silver Range Rover, with matching chrome spinners on the wheels. He stepped out looking clean in an Azzure tracksuit with a fresh pair of all white S. Carters on his feet. He was what most considered a pretty boy; bronze-toned skin, hazel eyes, and wavy hair that was bald faded on the sides. He had a nice physique due to the fact that he worked out several times a week. The lucky ladies that were blessed enough to be bedded by him found out he had a big muscle between his legs, as well as muscles on his arms.

As he approached the front door the aroma of his mother's fried chicken welcomed him. He walked into the house and called out, "hello, where is everyone?"

"Back here in the kitchen," his mother replied.

He went into the kitchen and gave his mom a kiss on her cheek.

"How's my favorite girl doing?" Marwan asked his mother. She smiled and replied, "I bet you say that to all the ladies." He sampled some of her mac' and cheese.

"Boy wait until dinner's done, and we're all sitting down at the table," she said.

After about another 20 minutes the food was done and the table was set. There was fried chicken, mac' and cheese, greens with cornmeal dumplings, rolls, and a carrot ring casserole.

"Marwan go call your siblings to the table so we can eat," said his mother.

Marwan went to the steps leading to the basement and yelled out, "Alexis and Mario come eat."

Yes, handsome, sexy, drug dealing Marwan was Rev. Davidson and Delores' 21 year-old son. After Marwan's siblings had finally come upstairs they each took turns embracing him. Delores and her children sat to the table. They'd grown accustomed to the Rev. staying after church for *official business*, and not joining them for Sunday dinner. Even though no one verbalized it, seeing his empty seat bothered them all.

Constantly living the fast life all week made Marwan deeply cherished these Sunday meals with his family; he knew it made his mother happy, and it also helped him to keep an eye on Alexis and Mario. The way Marwan was eyeing Alexis she knew what was coming next.

"So Lexi, you still kickin' it with that punk ass nigga?" asked Marwan.

"Boy, watch your mouth!" scolded Delores. Alexis rolled her eyes and sucked her teeth before she replied, "You wish you were half the man LeRoi is."

LeRoi was 20, and therefore in Marwan's eyes, too old for his only sister. It wasn't just the age thing that bothered him either. Marwan knew LeRoi was in the game just like him. He hated to think about it, but he knew hustlers only hung out with fine bitches that gave up the pussy. He didn't want to look at his sister in that light; but he knew that it was a fact of the game. That's why he never missed an opportunity to try to discourage Lexi from talking to niggas that were just like him. He knew she didn't hear it though.

Mario was a very quiet and introverted person. He was hard to read. Marwan decided from that day forward he would spend more time with him. Just earlier in the week Delores had called Marwan crying and fussing because she found an open box of condoms in Mario's room. Little did she know that Marwan set him up with his first piece of pussy on his fifteenth birthday. Nevertheless, he told his mom he would talk to him. Mario didn't say much, but he was very observant. He planned to get in the game just like his brother so he could floss too.

Before getting caught up in the game, Marwan was the typical pastor's child. He sang in the choir, worked in the youth department, and helped his father with whatever was needed. Like any other child he still got into mischief. When he was seventeen he impregnated the finest girl at the church, who was his then girlfriend. The Rev. did not want to bring reproach to the family's name, so he and Delores gave the girl's family some hush money (from the tithes and offerings), as well as paid for her abortion.

As Alexis and Mario cleaned away the dirty dishes and put the uneaten food away, Delores was lost in her thoughts. She wondered how and when her family became so dysfunctional. A husband that was unfaithful, a son who she suspected was involved in illegal activities, a daughter that acted loose, and a teenage son that was sexually active were just some of the issues that consumed her.

"Penny for your thoughts," said Marwan.

"I was just wondering how our family got so far off track. I tried to be the best wife and mother that I could. I raised my kids up in the fear and admonition of the Lord. I submitted myself to my husband like The Bible said to do. Now everything seems to have gone to shit!" exclaimed Delores. "I feel overwhelmed and depressed most of the time. I need you to be honest with me Marwan. Are you a drug pusher?"

Marwan was shocked, firstly because he had never heard his mother cuss before; secondly because her question was so blunt and in his face. As he sat there avoiding his mother's eyes and searching for the right words to say his Blackberry went off. *Saved by the fuckin' bell,* he thought.

"Sorry to end this, but I have to go mom."

She eyed him suspiciously and said, "That's just what I'm talking about."

He didn't want to end this day on bad terms, so he told her not to worry because everything would be fine with their family.

"It's just like the good book says 'train up a child in the way he should go, and when he is old he will not depart from it'," said Marwan.

This caused Delores' eyes to well up with tears, as he kissed her on the forehead and left.

"Nigga, I'm so glad you hit me up. My momma was about to get all up in my shit," said Marwan. His boy Shennon had hit him up on his cell phone.

"Playa where you at?" asked Shennon.

"Driving down Lahser. Headed to the spot on the eastside to pick up a package. Wanna roll wit' me?"

"Naw, I'm at Summerset Mall getting geared up for the party tonight," said Shennon.

Christian Coles, shooting guard for the Pistons, was throwing a big birthday bash at Club Ozone.

"Aight then, I'll holla at you later on," said Marwan before ending the call.

Marwan hopped on the 94 Freeway and came off on Harper. He then took that to Hyde St., which was located in the neighborhood called *The Bottoms*. This was named rightfully so because it was one of the worst areas in Detroit. He hopped out of his RR and set the alarm before walking up to the rundown house. After knocking on the door a few times, it opened, and let out a strong odor of *the green sticky*.

"Wassup my nigga?"

Marwan always felt funny whenever White Willie said that to him. No matter how down he was with the blacks, it just didn't seem right. He let it slide because White Willie had the cheapest price in the D for copping ecstasy to sell.

After he copped his work Marwan hooked up with a couple of his workers, so they could move the shit in the streets. After he dropped off the work he hopped back in his RR and called this freak he met the other day named Lola. Just the thought of her fine ass made his dick form a tent in his pants. Lola agreed to see him; so Marwan headed to her Riverfront condo downtown off E. Jefferson. Her lavish lifestyle was complements of her man who was on year two of a five year bid in the Ryan Correctional Facility.

When Lola opened the door for Marwan, he thought he was going to bust a nut right in his D&G boxers. She wore a tight ass, hot pink Juicy Couture tee. Barely covering her plump ass was a pair of matching hot pink terrycloth shorts, with Juicy written across the back in rhinestones. She had on a pair of pink 4-inch heel, Dior sandals that showed off her sexy feet with the American pedicure.

"Damn, you literally look good enough to eat," was Marwan's greeting.

"Well that explains your watering mouth," Lola said jokingly. He grabbed her and pulled her into him as they embraced. His tracksuit pants did nothing to conceal the hard-on that was poking her in the midsection.

After Marwan closed the door behind him with his foot, they sucked on each other's lips and tongues.
"Hello to you too," said Lola as he sucked on her neck and gripped those two hams in her shorts.

"Wassup baby doll," was Marwan's reply.

"Obviously this big ass dick you carrying around."

She put her hands on his chest and pushed him back from her. "I would appreciate a little conversation or something before you just start runnin' all up in me," stated Lola.

"That's my bad," said Marwan. "But what did you expect openin' the door lookin' all sexcellant and shit".

They both had to laugh at that. Lola made them some drinks, Hipnotiq and Bacardi Vanilla.

After they had a nice buzz and kicked it for a while, Lola stood up and motioned for Marwan to follow her to the bedroom. He heard the song *Naked* by R. Kelly start playing. By the time he made it in there she had taken off everything but her pumps. She lay back on her black and gold Versace bedspread and played with her pussy. Marwan licked his lips, stuck his hand in his boxers, and massaged his stiff dick. After completely stripping, Marwan climbed between Lola's legs face-first. Her pussy was fat and meaty, with a small amount of hair. He lapped up the juices from her wet pussy that her fingers had already stirred up.

"Oh my damn!" Lola exclaimed as she sucked on her sticky fingers.

He pulled her pussy lips apart and sucked and nibbled on her swollen clit. She came almost instantly, as lightening bolts shot through her body.

"Sounds like you up in here speaking in tongues," he chuckled.

After her body stopped twitching and convulsing, Marwan sucked on her erect nipples. Lola had two of the prettiest titties he'd ever seen.

"I don't know what the fuck it is about you, or if it's the liquor, but I wanna hit that shit raw-dog," said Marwan as he pinched her nipples.

"Nigga do what you want. Mi pussy is su pussy," she replied. That made him laugh.

Lola spread her legs apart and held them up, as Marwan guided his throbbing missile into her wet and ready sex box. She groaned from pleasure and pain. He groaned because her shit was tight and wet. As Marwan stroked her pussy with long deep strokes, Lola tightened her vaginal walls around his shit like a fist. The nigga was losing his mind up in her.

"Girl I need to bag yo' pussy up and sell it cause I'm sure it's better than any of them pills I'm pushin," Marwan said breathlessly.

Lola was coming again for the third time since he ran up in her. Strands of her honey-blonde straight hair were wet and stuck to her face.

Marwan's nut-sack tingled; so he knew he was about to bust.

"I'm bout to cum," he said.

"Let me drink that nut-shake," Lola begged.

He pulled out, grabbed her by the back of her hair, and stuffed his dick in her mouth. She sucked and slurped on his knob like her life depended on it. Marwan exploded in her mouth with a guttural yell. She swallowed his babies down, and then licked the slit in his dickhead. That made him shutter in ecstasy. Marwan was on the curious side; so he tongue kissed Lola to see what his nut tasted like.

After getting dressed and making plans to hook up again, Marwan bounced leaving Lola totally satisfied from his dick game.

-CHAPTER 4-

After he left Lola's, Marwan went to his Farmington Hills condo. It wasn't your normal bachelor pad. It was filled with top of the line everything including paintings from local upcoming artist Regina Mitchell. After he took a shower, he threw on a brand new Helmut Lang shirt and pants hookup. He then sprayed on his favorite cologne, Reaction by Kenneth Cole. Diamond studs, platinum Rolex, and a pair of big-block gators set the ensemble off. After checking himself over in the mirror for the umpteenth time he decided to give Shennon a call.

"Nigga, what's crackin'?"

"S.O.S," Shennon replied.

"Well let's go pop some bottles, and fuck some models," said Marwan.

"Nigga you know it's whatever," Shennon said, hyped up. He'd already smoked a blunt, and had two shots of Hennessy Privilege.

"Alright then, see you at the spot," Marwan said, before he ended the call.

Being raised in the church had always made him apprehensive of smoking weed, or trying any kind of drug that wasn't alcohol. He had no problem with selling the shit to others though.

After he went outside and hopped in his whip, he headed out to Club Ozone. When Marwan pulled up to the club he was treated like a celebrity. Valet rushed over to him opened his door, and treated him like a king. After he hanked the valet guy off with a fifty, Marwan strolled into the club like a runway model. It's a little early; but since there was going to be a lot of ballers and high rollers in the spot the females are already packed in. There was an open booth in a corner, so Marwan posted up in it. The honeys or vultures were already circling. Many he had fucked; and many he planned on fucking.

"What can I git yo fine ass tanite?" asked TaLunga the barmaid. "Wassup Ta Ta?"

"Let me just get a couple of bottles of Modelo Del Negro for now," said Marwan.

"I got yo Del Negro nigga. You need to quit fuckin' round with these snooty ass bitches, and get wit a ride or die bitch like me," said TaLunga, who considered that flirting.

After he looked at her electric blue and black tied zillions, along with her three gold hoops in each ear, Marwan almost broke out in laughter.

Instead he replied, "Girl you know you too much woman for me. Wit all dat ass, you gone have me spending all my money."
She did have a body made for fuckin' A nigga would just be ashamed to tell it afterwards.

After he drank one beer and started on the second, Marwan noticed a very sexy and mature female seated alone at the bar. He thought to himself that she would be one of his conquests for the night. The crew, Shennon, Russell, and Desmond finally arrived. They all slid in the booth and started talking about how much fine ass pussy was in the house.

"Damn, I feel like bending one of these bitches over, and fuckin' the shit out of them on this table!" yelled Russell.

"Shit. I'll take a good sloppy tongue lashing under the table right now," said Desmond.

They got TaLunga's attention, and ordered two bottles of Moet Brut.

After he finally recognized whom the lady at the bar was, Marwan decided to make his move. He got up, walked over to the bar, and then sat beside her.

"Shouldn't you be at church praying or something?" asked Marwan.

Startled, Theresa jumped and looked at him. She absentmindedly looked him up and down and licked her lips.

"Long time no see," she replied. "When are you going to stop by and visit your father's church?"

"Why should I, when I can just wait to see all the saints in the club?"

They both fell out laughing at his remark.

"You have really grown up to be a fine young man."

"I'm not a little boy anymore," said Marwan, as he grabbed his dick for emphasis.

"Don't play with me. I'm a grown ass woman, not one of these young hoochies," Theresa said, as she downed her second glass of White Zinfandel.

The DJ started playing a new track by a local singer named Becky J. Theresa danced in her seat, and said how she loved that song. Marwan took that as his cue, grabbed her hand, and led her to the dance floor. He was happy that it was a slow groove so he could pull her close, and grind on her. When they got to the center of the floor he lustfully looked her up and down, back and front. She knew she was killing it in her off-white Roberto Cavalli pants suit and red Manolo Blahnik stilettos. She wrapped her arms around his neck, and he pulled her in close by her waist. As Marwan rubbed up and down her back, he was totally enraptured by her fragrance.

"I love when a woman has on Pear Glace," he said.
She leaned her head back, looked in his eyes and asked how he knew. He wouldn't dare tell her that most of the strippers at Tiger's Lounge wore it. Instead he played it cool and told her that he only dealt with females that had good taste.

After slow grinding through two songs, the sexual tension between them became pretty thick. Her panties were moist and nipples hard. He had an erection that his European-cut trousers couldn't hide. Like father like son, she thought. There was an awkward silence between them as they strolled off the dance floor.

"Listen; thanks for the dance and company, but I think we should stop while we're ahead," Theresa said. "Stop what? All we did is dance. We didn't fuck like you and my father," said Marwan.

Although the wine had her tipsy, she knew she heard him clearly.

"What, you didn't think I knew?" he asked.

Theresa opened her mouth, but no words would come out. After the initial shock of his words, her embarrassment faded, thanks to the wine.

Why not have my cake and eat it too, she thought.

"Well, since you know about me and your father, what do you plan on doing with this information?" she asked.

He replied, "You should be asking what I plan on doing with your sexy ass."

Just then Shennon came over and interrupted them.

"Excuse me Casanova, but it's a few peeps that's asked if you got some 'E' they can cop."

"Yeah, tell them to meet by the bathrooms," said Marwan.

The way he and his boys dressed, Theresa knew Marwan was into something. Marwan pulled her close to him and told her to stay right there, because he had some business that needed to be handled.

-CHAPTER 5-

Since Delores decided to take the kids to see her mother in Hammond, IN, Rev. Davidson had the house to himself. He had already called Theresa several times, but got no answer. He figured she must still be fucked up from the party she went to last night.

"She betta' not had no young clown ass nigga up in my pussy," he said aloud to himself.

Not too long ago he knocked the shit out of her when he thought she was fucking around with Marty Holland – the church's Minister of Music. He had nothing to do, he figured he might as well turn on his laptop and prepare Sunday's sermon.

After he sat and stared at a blank screen for a while, Rev Davidson acknowledged that he needed a little inspiration. So he went and retrieved his half empty fifth of Jack Daniels and a glass. After he drank what amounted to two double shots he felt more devilish than angelic.

"The sermon can wait 'till later," he said to no one.

A few keystrokes later, and he was at his favorite Internet porn site. He logged on to *Barely Legal Black Babes*, and stripped down to his tightee whites. He figured he might as well have some personal fornication since he was alone. After he keyed in his screen name (Holy Hoe), he was in the chat room, drunk as he got his cyber-freak on.

-CHAPTER 6-

It had been a little over a week since Theresa hooked up with Marwan at Club Ozone. Ever since then he had hooked her up with a steady supply of ecstasy and dick. She knew that she gave it as good as she got it, because he paid up her rent and car note for the next 6 months. The Rev. usually took care of those expenses. So she'd take the bread that he gave her and stack it up in her account. Theresa knew she'd been neglecting The Rev., so she gave him a call.

"Hey baby."

"Don't hey baby me bitch!" he angrily replied. "Why the fuck haven't you been returning my calls? I know you met some ball player or dope dealing punk at that party. That's why you've been MIA. All of a sudden the church's money ain't enough for you? You think them young niggas want yo old ass? Bitch please! You betta stick wit' what you know – and that's me," he ranted.

She knew this was coming, so she wasn't shocked. Even though his words angered her, she kept her mouth shut, because he was steady money and dick for her.

"You're right daddy," was all she responded with.

"Damn right I'm right. Now when am I gonna see you?"

"Why don't you go to Stanley's, pick up some Chinese food, and come on over so I can show you how truly sorry I am," she meekly replied.

Within that same hour The Rev. sat at Theresa's table, eating shrimp in lobster sauce over rice, while he got his dick sucked.

After Theresa satisfied her appetite with Chinese food and dick, she decided to have a serious talk with her lover.

"Elias, do you ever think about leaving Delores for me?"

He asked, "Now why you wanna go and fuck up a good evening with some dumb bullshit like that? You know I'm not leaving my wife. Plus, you could never be *first lady* material."

"Get the fuck out you asshole!" she screamed as tears streamed down her face.

He simply laughed, stood up, and said, "I'll call you tomorrow and you had better answer."

After The Rev. was gone Theresa felt she needed a hallucinogen to help her escape the evening's madness. She called Marwan and told him she needed a fix. He assumed she meant dick, but she quickly set him straight. He told her he was hanging at the club with his boys and to meet him there. She grabbed her keys and Marc Jacobs bag and headed out the door. She was in such a hurry that she didn't notice The Rev.'s Escalade still parked across the street. When he saw Theresa bolt out of her driveway his inquisitive mind got the best of him; so he followed her.

-CHAPTER 7-

After he got the call from Theresa, Marwan resumed partying with his crew. He was drinking Moet straight out the bottle and spitting mad game to this fine chick in VIP. The drunken female was giving him a lap dance like it's a titty bar. She rubbed her ass all over his dick and had Marwan about to bust a nut right in his Sean John cargo pants. The vibration of his phone interrupted the moment of pleasure. He removed the girl from his lap; and told her he had some business to handle. She told him to hurry back, as she yanked on his woody.

As he walked outside, Marwan spotted Theresa's Cherokee. She saw him approach her ride, and got out.

"Ma, why you lookin' so upset?" inquired Marwan.

"It's nothing I want to go into right now," she said.

Being the ever-horny nigga that he was, he licked his lips and stated, "I would love to go into that pussy right now, though."

She let out a fake chuckle, and lied; telling him that she just came on.

Unnoticed in his truck, The Rev. watched the whole scene, as a thousand thoughts ran through his head. He watched as Marwan retrieved something from his pocket, and passed it to Theresa. She then hugged him as he palmed both of her ass cheeks. They were locked in an intimate kiss that enabled them from seeing The Rev. approach with a gun at his side.

"So just what the fuck do we have here?!" yelled the deliriously mad reverend.

Caught by total surprise the mistress and the son stood there speechless.

"What's wrong son; pussy got your tongue?"

The Rev. glared at Theresa and said, "I knew you was fuckin' around wit' some young, dumb ass nigga you met here; but I never guessed it would be the one that I shot out my own nut-sac!."

"Look Pops, you need to chill out. How the fuck you gonna be mad and you the one that's cheating on yo' wife – my mother," said Marwan.

The Rev. raised his gun at Marwan and said, "You stupid little shit. You've always been a mama's boy. Whenever I wanted to whup yo' ass you would run to her for protection. Well she ain't here to save you now."

Theresa finally spoke up and said, "Elias, think about what you're saying and doing. He's your own flesh and blood."
"Well, your triflin' ass should have thought about that before you started fuckin' him" he responded.

While his father's attention was off of him, Marwan saw that as his chance to get the gun from his pops.

As Marwan lunged at him, The Rev saw him in his peripheral view, and reflexively pulled the trigger. Suddenly there was a hole in the middle of Marwan's forehead as he fell backwards. Blood, skull fragments, and brain matter came out the back of his head, and splattered Theresa's face and clothes. She let out a blood-curdling scream and fell to her knees. Marwan was dead before he hit the ground. Some of the club patrons witnessed the shooting, and used their cell phones to call for an ambulance.

While Theresa was on the ground wailing and pleading for Marwan not to die, The Rev. stood over both of them, numb and in a state of shock. A small crowd started to gather around the grisly scene. A young cat noticed Marwan lying dead, and ran inside to get his boys. The faint sound of sirens grew louder and closer in the distance.

After what felt like an eternity to him, The Rev. bowed on his knees, moved Theresa out the way, and cradled his son's lifeless body. Tears streamed down his face as his lips quivered. He looked up in the starry sky and said, "Father forgive me for I know not what I've done!"

With that said he took the gun, put it in his mouth, and pulled the trigger.

-CHAPTER 8-

The day was cold, grey, and rainy. It was as if God set the perfect backdrop for today's double funeral. Since there would be so many mourners in attendance, the service was held at Greater Word of Grace Cathedral of High Praise. There was a seemingly endless line of people coming to pay their respects to two men whose lives ended so tragically. There were all kinds of floral arrangements surrounding the Mahogany caskets. The Mega Mass Voices of Faith Choir sang song after song during the wake.

Even as they mourned, Shennon, Russell, and Desmond – along with every other male in the church – couldn't help but notice how many top of the line females paraded around to view the bodies. That did not go unnoticed by Delores either. Through her sobs she silently wondered how many of them were there because they had either been fucked by her husband or her son.

All of a sudden a certain vibe or energy could be felt throughout the church. That was because Theresa had just entered and shocked everyone. No one believed she had the balls to show up, but she did. She strutted in dressed to kill; with her black pinstriped Dolce & Gabbana suit, Bottega Veneta boots, Kate Spade bag, and Jackie O. shades.

"That bitch got some nerve," one attendee said.

There were similar sentiments like that all over the congregation. Theresa knew all eyes were on her, but she didn't give a damn. Her heart truly ached. In one night she lost the man she loved; and the young man she loved to fuck. As she stood over Rev. Davidson's body she wanted so bad to lean over and plant a kiss on his cheek, but thought better of it. She however did kiss Marwan.

"Get your filthy lips off my son you tramp!" screamed Delores. Alexis, Mario, and others had to restrain her from jumping on Theresa. After Theresa left out, and things quieted down, Mario sat there thought to himself. Instead of hating Theresa like the women in his family, he had a hard-on for her like the men. Maybe she'd keep it in the family, he thought to himself.

Alexis tried to console her mother by telling her not to worry, because she had plans for Theresa. While Theresa was in the church, one of the plans had materialized. Alexis had some of her girls on the lookout for Theresa's Cherokee in case she did decide to show up to the funeral. After Theresa entered the church, the females took a bat to all of her windows, punctured all of her tires, and spray painted all kinds of vulgar and obscene words on her truck. By the time she exited the church they were long gone.

-CHAPTER 9-

It was a week after the funeral and Theresa was in bed crying and depressed. After the manslaughter/suicide she couldn't keep any food on her stomach. She went to her doctor hoping she would be prescribed some type of pills for post-traumatic stress. After some tests were run, the doctor informed her that her vomiting was due to the fact that she was pregnant.

Since she received the news all Theresa did was cry and sleep. There was no way to tell whom the father was; because both men she had been sleeping with were six feet underground. She had no vehicle, no steady income, and no will to live anymore.

Theresa heard someone steadily knocking on her front door, and ringing the bell. She assumed it was Jehovah Witnesses, and wished they would go away. After three minutes went by, and the noise persisted, Theresa went to answer the door ready to cuss out whoever was on the other side of it. She flung the door open and was totally surprised by her visitor.

"Well, well. Don't you look a hot mess," remarked Deacon Ellis. "I guess being a hoe took its toll on you."

"Did you drive your limp dick, impotent ass over here just to insult me, or is there a reason for your visit?" she asked.

"Yes there is a reason," he stated. "You must have sunshine pussy like ol' girl in that movie. The deacon board went through the churches financial papers, and came across something very interesting."

Oblivious to what he was talking about Theresa just glared at him annoyed. He cleared his throat and continued.

"It seems our pastor and overseer, the late Rev. Elias Davidson has left the church and everything belonging to it in your name."
It took a minute for it all to register in Theresa's spinning head.

Deacon Ellis continued on, "This includes his new Escalade that we've parked in front of your place. Here are the keys, deeds, and titles to everything."

With this all said Deacon Ellis turned and left.

Still totally amazed, Theresa slid down her wall until she was sitting on the floor. Holding the keys and papers to her bright future, she looked up at the ceiling and said, "God, I guess you do work in mysterious ways."

Family Affairs

Written by: Anthony Striggles

-Chapter One-

The Mercury Theatre is abuzz with activity as hundreds of adolescents congregate to view the movie about a giant shark. Eddie can't wait until he and Joan Perry are hugged up close together in their seats. Eddie has already determined that he would try his hand at fingering her tonight; he's pleased that she opted to wear a miniskirt.

"Why does your Pops wig out on me so much these days", Eddie asks Joan. "Does he know we've been fooling around?"

"I don't know, but he and my mother have been telling me that you and I spend too much time together," Joan says as she shrugs.

"Sometimes I really hate being a Pastor's kid, so many damn rules. They're always talking about 'our image."

"Yeah, I'm hip Joan! You know next week is my Dad's Appreciation Services. Anyway, I want to go to that *"DeBarge"* and *"Ready For The World"* concert down at Ford Auditorium. But my Old G is like 'How is it going to look if Reverend Edward Majors' only son isn't present at a service in honor of his father?' I told her that his Appreciation was a whole week, and my missing one night wouldn't matter. But you know that shit didn't wash with her."

"Ooh, they make me sick! I had to sneak here tonight. My folks think I 'm with Yolanda and her lame ass crew over at the State Fair Bowl."

"Joan, your little sister is pretty nerdy", Eddie says as he lets out a bellow of laughter.

"Yeah, but that's my ace."

Eddie purchases a large popcorn and two medium grape Nehi sodas before he and Joan are seated in the theatre. As soon as the lights are dimmed, Eddie is pressing the offensive to put his hands in places he's never seen.

Before the first screams of terror are emitted by Mandible's first victim, Joan's legs are parted and Eddie is rubbing her mound as if attempting to spark a fire, so with some assistance, he finally finds the Promised Land.

After thoroughly tickling Joan's fancy, Eddie's fingers weren't the only parts of his anatomy to get wet that night. No, indeed the night held more firsts for both he and Joan.

-Chapter 2-

Staring at all of the plaques and certificates on the walls, Eddie's desire is to be as great as his father is. This particular fire has been burning since he was a lad. The respect and honor showed his father, borders on worship.

The Reverend Edward D. Majors is a man among men in the city of Detroit. His flourishing church has been a central thread in the Motor City's fabric for almost two decades.

Edward Jr. sits patiently before his father, as he concludes an urgent phone conversation with the current City Council President. He's given the one moment gesture, so he continues to scan the room. He looks at the framed picture of his father speaking at a press conference after the Riots of '68. His eyes then fall on the family portrait that's directly in front of him. The warm photo of Reverend and Mrs. Majors with their two children looks so serene.

Young Eddie's attention is arrested as Rev. Majors places the telephone into its cradle. The Reverend proceeds to broach a topic that has been much discussed in their household. Mr. and Mrs. Majors are concerned about Eddie's choice in women, particularly his current girlfriend.

After Joan's father relocated the family to California, Eddie began dating regularly. While the Right Reverend hasn't voiced his displeasure to his son, his wife and Eddie's sister fire away at will. His ire is raised at his namesake because Rachelle has told several members of the congregation that she and Eddie have been rendezvousing at the Blue Bird Motel.

"Eddie, I perhaps more than anyone, realize that we as men have certain needs. It's not the *what* that was wrong, it's the *how* that we need to discuss. I want, no I need for you to be more sound in your decision making son", Reverend Edward Majors Sr. tells Eddie. He explains to his son the merits and necessity of being both discriminate and discreet.

When the two-hour lecture is over, the young man Majors has learned that a roaring lion is not the one to be feared. In fact, that lion, is usually a decoy, used to scare would-be prey, and send them scurrying off in the direction of the silent killer, the lioness.

The illustration was dual in nature. First, it was another way of saying that the emptiest wagon makes the most noise. But more importantly, it showed the power of a silent, stealthy woman.

Eddie really appreciated his father imparting that kind of wisdom to him. He used those same principles in choosing the lady that has been part of his life for the past ten years.

Unfortunately, Loretta isn't his wife. No, Edward didn't comprehend what his dad was saying until after he married his girlfriend. His was an error that is regretted daily, and the injury was insulted by the birth of a son in the first year of marriage. Although Eddie loves E3 with every fiber of his being, he just wished that his son's mother, were someone that he could, or rather, wanted to love.

-CHAPTER 3-

Rita was an ambitious young woman. It only took one conversation with Edward Jr. for her to realize his great naiveté. He was dating another girl in the congregation when she made her play for him.

Church was a lot like school in regards to rumors and gossip. The word on Eddie was that he was just beginning to have sex. His mother kept him on a very short leash, because she knew that the young girls in the church were hot-n-readies.

The church's youth group had an outing at Edgewater Park, and Rita instructed her best friend to leave her so that she could play the damsel in distress. The unwitting church boy took a bite of the fruit.

Eddie had perks being a PK (Pastor's Kid), and one of them was his gray Cadillac Cimarron. Rita settled into the passenger's seat, as if she came with the car. She suggested they stop at Farrell's for some root beer floats. Eddie agreed quickly.

After an hour of conversation, he was wide open. Their first date was the following weekend. After the movie, they went to Belle Isle and engaged in some very heavy petting. Rita worked young Eddie like sweat-shop owner. When his jeans were almost creamy, she pushed him away and said that she wasn't going to give herself to him on the first date. But, as a consolation prize, she would give him some head. Edward Majors Jr. broke up with Rachelle that night.

Rita, to be so young, was well-versed in church politics. Her uncle was the Brotherhood Chairman at the church, and spoke often of how Eddie was being groomed to take his father's throne, so Rita waited until she was pretty certain that that would be the case before putting her scheme into motion.

Rita envisioned herself being First Lady of one of the most prominent churches in all of Detroit, and was willing to do whatever it took to make it happen. Luckily for her, her feminine wiles were more than a match for Eddie. She dangled the prospect of sex in front of him for a couple of weeks before giving in to him.

Eddie's parents never said anything to Rita, but his mother would give her the "you low-bitch" stare quite frequently. When Rita would question him about it, his response was always music to her ears. He was his own man.

After graduation, Eddie got prepared to go into the family business, so he enrolled at the Michigan Theological Seminary. This pleased his father immensely. Eddie learned Church Government and History, Eschatology, Hermeneutics, Homiletics, Ministerial Ethics, and Theology.

He was into his 3rd year when Rita began the "we need to get married" song and dance. She had sagely begun to cut down on the frequency of their sexual encounters. It was a ploy that worked masterfully.

So, in the fall of '78, Edward and Rita were engaged. Mrs. Majors decided to take an active roll in grooming her future daughter-in-law for the crown she would one day where.

Eddie concentrated on his final year of school, while Rita and her mother planned the wedding. After he walked across the stage in May, Rita and Eddie were wed in September.

Mrs. Rita Majors wasted no time conceiving, for she knew that that would be the finishing stroke on the masterpiece she'd painted for herself.

Rita gave birth to their first child in July of '79. Edward Majors III was the spitting image of his father. Not just in appearance, but his personality also mirrored Eddie.

The grandparents spoiled him to no end. Grand Pa Majors inwardly rejoiced that his name would be carried on at least one more generation, effectively cementing the Majors' legacy in the history of Detroit.

Two years later, Rita and Eddie had their second child, another boy. Marc-Anthony embodied the spirit of his mother, very cunning and shrewd. Rita had her tubes tied after giving birth to Marc-Anthony. Her need to breed had been satisfied, and she was determined to maintain her size 6 figure.

-Chapter 4-

Loretta joined the Faith Fellowship Congregational Church at
the beginning of '85. Her son and Edward Majors III were in
kindergarten together the previous year. Now Calvin and E3 were
inseparable as first-graders. Rita Majors and Loretta were both
very active in the PTA. Due to the children's connection and their
interactions in the PTA, the two women became friends. So it was
only natural that Loretta and Calvin found themselves at FFCC.

Calvin's dad had been served papers of divorcement when the
lad was but two years old. Mr. Roberts suffered from Penile
Indiscretion Syndrome, or PIS.

Loretta, having been PIS-ed upon one time too many, got the
house, a car, and a sizable amount of money not to disclose her
husband's extramarital activities to anyone. This was in addition to
child support for little Calvin. Warren Roberts was a Man of the
Cloth, and being the chairman of the Minister's Alliance of
Southeast Michigan, could afford no public scandal.

Loretta Roberts quickly became an active member of Faith
Fellowship Christian Church. Her spirited and soulful singing was
received as if Manna from Heaven. Loretta also transitioned
herself into the church's business, and became the Head
Administrator, her business savvy proved to be invaluable.

Meanwhile, Eddie Jr. had been promoted to Assistant Pastor,
and together he and Loretta made a formidable duo. They took the
church into previously unexplored areas of media, and with the

advent of Christian Broadcasting on Cable and Satellite Television, Reverend Edward Majors Sr. was recognized nationally.

Loretta threw herself into her work, every task or project was given her level best. This allowed her an escape from the emptiness that was her life. Loretta's hard work was rewarded by an offer to become a full-time salaried employee of the Faith Fellowship Christian Church.

During this time, Eddie became attracted to Loretta. He was often caught gazing longingly into her pretty brown eyes, and wondering if her milk chocolate colored skin was as soft, and tasted as sweet as it looked.

-Chapter 5-

The 90's began with much excitement. The Pistons won their first two World Championships back to back. Barry Sanders was amazing the free world with his improbable running. The Bad Boys, and Thumbs Up, became part of the social fabric of Detroit. The Red Wings began their assent into the upper echelon of Professional Hockey led by "another Stevie", and he changed *Motown* into *Hockeytown*. Octopus sales began to rise dramatically in May and June. Unfortunately, the Tigers did nothing but change the official team pizza. Detroit's baseball team went from *Avoid the Noid*, to a miniature caricature of Greek royalty.

The new decade brought with it a fresh enthusiasm and feeling of promise to Eddie. He finally found his lane. This self-realization fostered a confidence that burned like a super-nova. His quiet yet powerful presence endeared him to all of the parishioners. As Co-Pastor, his was a job that required quite a bit of interaction with the people. Counseling turned out to be his forte. Pastor Eddie became known for his sound judgment, with wisdom that exceeded his years. Meanwhile, Reverend Majors' health began to decline, so Eddie assumed more and more of the pastorate. And as the church membership blossomed and grew, so did the chasm between Rita and Eddie.

Eddie and Rita's obvious lack of a connection caused Eddie's parents to question him as to the state of the marriage. He tried to reassure them that all was well, but his parents, who were no dummies, knew better. They had already privately discussed the apparent lack of affection between their son and daughter-in-law.

One faithful day, while at lunch, Eddie daringly tells Loretta of his attraction to her. "Eddie, I definitely feel the same for you, and have for some time." Urged on by her response, he explores the possibility of them acting on their desires.

"But Eddie, you know that Rita and I are close. Not to mention that our sons are best friends."

Eddie assured Loretta that they would be as discreet as humanly possible. Thus began the most meaningful relationship of Eddie's life.

-CHAPTER 6-

Loretta felt extremely guilty about her feelings for Eddie until one day while sipping strawberry margaritas at lunch with Rita. The girls decided to go to Mexican Town and it was there, where Eddie's wife admitted that she never really loved him, but married him only to better herself.

Her justification was that marriage was instituted as law for the purpose of land ownership. In other words, if a man died without any heirs, his property wouldn't be forfeit to the government. So according to Rita, love never had anything to do with it. Hell, men were marrying for status all the time, so why shouldn't she?

"Loretta, it's a dog-eat-dog world, so a bitch had best sharpen her teeth", was Rita's rationale.

Near the bottom of the second pitcher of margaritas, Rita confides to Loretta that she's been involved with Deacon Horton, who was head of the Official Board at Faith Fellowship Christian Church. Loretta was shocked, not that Deacon Horton would cheat on his wife, but that Rita would allow herself to be involved with a womanizer like him. He was screwing everything that wasn't nailed down in the church.

Deacon Horton had been brought before Reverend Majors several times due to his wayward penis. Each time, he was exonerated of all wrongdoing due to a "lack of proof." Evidently, taped phone conversations and being caught with one's dick in the nookie jar was just circumstantial evidence against the top tither of FFCC.

It was at this point that Loretta decided that Eddie deserved better than Rita, and she was just the woman to give it to him. Loretta already had an airtight alibi for spending time with Eddie. Her position at the church gave Eddie and Loretta many days and nights together. Rita was more than glad to have Eddie's responsibilities keep him away from home. It gave her more time to be a socialite, and release her inner freak with Deacon Horton whose kink-meter was apparently broken.

When I've gone the last mile of the way, I shall rest at the close of the day. And I know there is peace that awaits me, when I've gone the last mile of the way. Edward Majors Jr. had sung those words, countless times, but the poetic finality of this death-carol gives him pause.

Eddie really isn't hearing any of the well-wishes or condolences of the thousands of mourners that stream by to pay their respects to the late Rev. Edward Majors Sr. His thoughts are of the many pleasant childhood memories shared with his father. Ironically, none of them involved the church, it's at this moment that he realizes he has to forge a bond with his sons outside of the four walls of FFCC. Eddie hopes it isn't too late for them. He has been too consumed with the business of church, that and Loretta Roberts.

Pastor Majors is said with such reverence, it rivals the scene in the *Godfather* when Michael takes over the Corleone Family. Eddie's butt has passion marks on both cheeks from all of the ass-kissers in attendance. He recalls the wise words of Rev. Majors while watching a Pistons game one night. "Junior, Zeke is the best Point Guard in the league because he's so alert, a true floor general. You should remember to always keep your head up, that way, you can always see the bullshit coming."

The funeral scene is rather surreal. Seated to his right, Eddie's mother weeps silently. It's a controlled cry, not one of wracking grief. It's certainly not a cry that speaks of 48 years of marriage.

Turning to his left he surveys his wife Rita. Eddie is sickened by her Oscar-worthy performance. He decides that if she doubles over again wailing, he'll just push her to the floor. He loathes himself for falling for the first woman to orally pleasure him. But Eddie is pleased that he was able to conceal the fact that he was now a multi-millionaire from his parasite of a wife.

The late Reverend Majors had quite a life insurance policy. Mrs. Majors received five million dollars, while LaVerne, Eddie's older sister, and Eddie received three million apiece. Eddie's very capable accountant hid his inheritance in an offshore account in Ontario, Canada.

E3 and Marc-Anthony seem to be holding up pretty well. Eddie notices one of the ushers as she flirtatiously smiles at Marc-Anthony. He saw something in his youngest son's eyes that worried him. It was the look of a hunter. While inwardly proud of his offspring, being that the young woman was quite a looker, Eddie knows he has to have a *man-to-boy* with Marc-Anthony.

LaVerne and her husband are seated on the other side of the Majors boys. Eddie looked at Karl with disgust. He wonders how and why his sister would willingly stay with a *nut-juggler*. Karl had been caught on his knees in Palmer Park, a known hangout of gay men. The officer who happened upon the two men, being a member of Faith Fellowship Christian Church, recognized Karl immediately, so no tickets were issued.

Eddie figured that that would have caused Karl to straighten up and fly right, but no, Karl is an incorrigible cocksucker.

After a fit of guilt, the youth pastor of FFCC confessed to Rev. Majors that he and Karl had been intimates. To wit, Rev. Majors was heard yelling to Karl in a closed-door meeting that "he was not to suck another dick in the church!".

Pastor Edward Majors Jr. adjusts his grey monochromatic Givenchy tie moments before the emcee of the funeral service announces him. The grey Roberto Cavalli four-button single-breasted suit and crisp white shirt are impeccably tailored. The smoke grey big-block gators on his feet are worn in true Detroit fashion.

"First of all, on behalf of the Majors family, I want to thank all of you who have come from far and near to honor the memory of the greatest man that I've ever known." Eddie pauses until the thunderous applause dissipates. I want to especially thank my good friend and brother, Stan Jones for that electrifying song. *You Are* is, or rather, was my father's favorite song."

Eddie's eulogy is short and succinct. While speaking he looks around the packed auditorium, and swells with pride at his inherited empire.

-Chapter 8-

Loretta was really working it. The years of Kegal exercises were having the desired effect as she road him to ecstasy. Loretta's vaginal muscles held Eddie's penis in what she liked to call the *Glory Grip*. Eddie's moans of pleasure and unintelligible babbling made it sound as if he were speaking in tongues. She loved the fact that after all of these years, she still had this effect on him.

As the two lovers lie spent next to each other, there rests a thick silence between them. It's the foreboding and familiar cloud of an argument had many times in the past. Eddie waits patiently for the storm to erupt.

"Eddie, you know you mean the world to me." This is all just a lead-in to the real issue at hand. Eddie inhales deeply right before he's asked when he will divorce his bitch-of-a-wife. Loretta is none too pleased as he explains to her how bad it would look for a man in his position to divorce his wife.

"Eddie, pastors are getting divorced all the time these days. It's not as taboo as you're making it out to be." Loretta sites a certain preacher in California that divorced his wife, and married his secretary a week later. "His ministry is still thriving."

"Babe, this isn't Hollyweird, it's Detroit. People tend to be less forgiving. If I'm going to be in the *Free Press*, I'd rather that not be the reason", Eddie says attempting to smooth her ruffled feathers.

Loretta, not to be put off, brings up a Grammy-award winning Recording Artist turned pastor who divorced his wife, and now is enjoying great success on the Westside of Detroit. This point hits home with Eddie. He closes his eyes and pauses for a moment before responding. Edward Majors Jr. knows that he has to choose his words carefully.

"Loretta, I love you more than I can truly verbalize. And I would like nothing more than to be able to do it with no limits. But, as a Spiritual Leader and Role Model, it would send the wrong message if I divorced Rita and married you."

This of course, doesn't sit well with Ms. Roberts.

"So, I'm good enough to bed for years, but not good enough for you to commit to?"

"Baby, I don't want you to feel like that. I could not be who or where I am right now without your support." Eddie embraces his mistress and caresses her face. "Loretta the key to my longevity is to present at least what appears to be a stable home life." For that reason, Eddie tells Loretta that he is duty-bound to continue his charade with Rita.

-Chapter 9-

The silence is deafening. No one moves or says anything for several extremely awkward moments. Eddie's mother has just revealed that she has accepted the marriage proposal of their father's long-time friend, Reverend Ellis Perry, and that she'll be relocating to the West Coast. Eddie is irate, because his dad has only been in the ground for a bit more than ninety days.

None of Ms. Majors' rationale suffices, so Eddie proceeds down a road he is unprepared to navigate. "How can you do this so soon? It's like dad meant nothing to you."

"He meant the world to me, but you should know, Edward only married me because I was pregnant with you LaVerne. He took great joy in telling me this whenever the mood struck him.

LaVerne wept like a baby, while Eddie sat powerless as the pedestal of integrity his father sat upon began to crumble.

Ms. Majors admitted that she knew that two wrongs didn't equal a right, and that her actions weren't about revenge. "Ellis actually makes me happy. I just hope that you two can be happy for and with me."

Visibly shaken, Ms. Majors' eldest child leaves without a word. She then turns to her son whose pain-filled eyes are trained on her. "I'm glad she's gone so she won't hear what I have to say next."

Eddie braces himself. "Son, you of all people should understand me. I know you don't actually believe no one knows about you and Loretta Roberts." Eddie's mouth opens, but no words exit.

Upon gathering himself, his *Male Defense System* kicks in. "I don't know what you're talking about; there's nothing between Loretta and I."

Ms. Majors looks pensively at her son and says, "Your father has taught you well, but what you don't know, is I'm the one who taught your father." Confused, Eddie waits for an explanation. "I walked in on Edward as he was down-stroking into Sister McGee just one week after we married." Eddie sat with his mouth agape as his ears were assaulted by the revelation of his father being with the woman he affectionately referred to as *Aunt Audrey*.

"How…why did you stay with him?"

"Because I loved your father. His charisma was magnetic, and when I saw the potential he had as a young minister, I was determined to remain at his side. As I'm sure you've discovered, women are attracted to power, and your father had a type of electricity about him that was undeniable."

"So you were willing to put up with his infidelity for status?" "That's not just it. Black folk just didn't up and get divorced back then, we toughed it out. To us, *For Better or For Worse* really carried weight; it's these Oprah-generation women who divorce at the first sign of trouble."

"I need a drink", Eddie says as he rises and strides uneasily to the wet bar on the other side of the room. He rarely drinks in front of his mother, but a double shot of Bombay Sapphire Gin is definitely in order. He downs it dry in two gulps, and pours himself a second dosage before returning to his mother.

"I'm not telling you this to sully your father's memory, my reason is to prepare and warn you for the eventuality of you having to deal with your own waywardness Eddie."

"But..." he says until Ms. Majors raises her hand, effectively cutting off his attempt at denial. Inwardly, Eddie is glad that he doesn't have to lie to his mother's face again.

"Eddie, there are things that your Dad and I, that we, have kept from you for far too long."

"Mom, I don't know if I want to hear any more." Undaunted, she presses on.

"Eddie... Ellis Perry is your biological father."

Edward Majors Jr. is reeling from his mother's confessions; he looks at her pleadingly as if she would just say it was all a hoax. Instead, she reaches out and takes his glass, downing its contents in one throat-searing gulp.

Eddie replays the admonishing of Edward Sr. to beware of the indiscreet woman. He suddenly realized that the silent and deadly lioness that he spoke of was sitting right across from him.

"Does Uncle…, does he know?"

"Yes, he knows", Ms. Majors says unflinchingly. "The three of us decided…"

"*The three of you*? So dad knew all along..."

"Your father…, Edward discovered my affair, and was devastated. For some reason, you men seem to think that turnabout is not fair play. And hear me; I never intended to cheat on your…, on Edward. It's just that Ellis was the one person that I felt I could tell anything to, and not be condemned. That level of intimacy is almost always coupled with physical intimacy."

He halts his mother, not wanting to hear of her sexing. Eddie stands and strolls around the room with his hands clasped atop his head. The Bombay that's exiting his pores has caused a thin sheet of perspiration to form along his furrowed brow.

"How could he have gone to his grave without telling me?"

As much as she can, Mattie King Majors consoles her son. "Eddie, your dad saw you not as a constant reminder of our failed commitment to each other, because he loved you as his own. Although he didn't seed you, Edward felt that his misdeeds directly caused your conception, for he pushed me to the arms of another."

"Damn, my entire life is a lie!" Eddie says dejectedly as he grabs another glass and the bottle of Bombay. "So only the three of you know of my secret identity?"

"Ellis told his wife, and she respected his wishes to remain silent about it."

"They sure don't make 'em like you all anymore. She died with the secret too?", Eddie says speaking of the late Mrs. Ellis Perry.

Suddenly, like a jolt of 50,000 volts, a realization hits Eddie. He drops onto the couch like a sack of potatoes.

"I know this is a lot to digest son, and I'm sorry you had to hear it like this. But sometimes things happen in life that we don't plan for, we have to just try and make the best of it."

When Eddie doesn't respond, Ms. Majors looks over at him. His eyes are glazed, and he appears to be a million miles away from Rosedale Park.

"So she's my sister! Joan and Yolanda are my sisters!"

"Yes Eddie. We didn't want you all to grow up and not at least know each other."

"Do you know what you've done?" he yells while rocketing off of the couch. "Now I know why they moved to Corona so suddenly. That church was just a convenient excuse. You all found out that Joan and I had been having sex!" He returns to the bar and picks up the peppery gin. Eddie gulps until his chest hairs smolder.

Not being able to make eye contact with him, Mattie says, "None of us wanted that to happen. That's why we tried to keep you separated as much as possible. We saw where you were headed." "But keeping the secret was more important than stopping us from committing incest", he says bitterly.

"Eddie, son you have to know..."

"Mother, you've said quite enough today. I just wish you could have been this chatty when it mattered most."

Eddie wobbles toward the door and wonders if it's the gin he's consumed or the disconcerting information that has him so tilted. He pauses at the door before leaving. "As far as I'm concerned, you died with Dad. I never want to speak to you again", Eddie says without turning around.

-CHAPTER 11-

"I brought the *Astro-Glide* tonight", she says lewdly as he closes the hotel room door.

"Well, then that makes it worth the trip. I don't know why we have to come way out here to Warren just to get a room", Deacon Leon Horton complains.

"You know how *we* are", referring to Black Motorists in Detroit. We ain't crossing 8 Mile unless we absolutely have to, and that's before sundown. The likelihood of any of the saints seein' us out here is very slim", First Lady Rita Majors explains. "Now get over here and give me some of that tongue language."

"Ain't nuttin' but a word woman, you know me, elbows, toes and assholes, I touch em' all", he says as he flicks his ridiculously long tongue out and touches his nose. Deacon Horton quickly undresses and joins Rita in bed.

Half an hour later, the two lovers are ready for round two. "Does Pastor Eddie know what a freak he's married to?" he asks while lubricating Rita's anus.

"Does your wife like the way my coochie tastes when she's kissing you?" Nothing but groans and moans exit the lips of Rita and Leon the rest of their stay.

-CHAPTER 12-

"Ok Karl, I'll see you in an hour," Eddie says as he hangs up the phone. "I wonder what this is about?" he says aloud to himself. He then buzzes his secretary. "Phyllis, will you please call Bishop Roberts and tell him that unfortunately, we'll have to reschedule?"

Tell him to just say when and where, and I'm there. Thank you.

And you can have the rest of the day off, I'm leaving and won't be returning."

Eddie hasn't shared with anyone the fact that his father is actually alive and well in Southern California. Nor the fact that he and his half-sister lost their virginity to each other. He considered calling Joan and Yolanda, but couldn't quite decide on how to broach the subject.

Forty-five minutes later, Eddie parks his Grey Audi A8 across the street from Fishbones and pays the parking lot attendant. He always loves lunchtime in Greektown. All of the corporate honeys scurrying about are a thing of beauty. As he crosses Monroe appreciating the business end of the navy blue mid-thigh skirt that sashayed before him, Eddie thinks to himself about how many fine women he sees daily in Detroit and the Metro Area.

Whether at the cleaners, or the neighborhood Coney Island, he's guaranteed to see a woman that makes him thank God for His creation.

"I already got us a table Eddie", Karl says snatching Eddie from his happy place. Eddie smiles at the cute little hostess at the entrance as he follows Karl to the table.

"Ok, what's the deal Karl?" he asks. "You've never demanded a sit down with me before."

"Direct and to the point as always Eddie. I came to you because as my pastor and brother-in-law, you've always treated me with respect even though you knew I was living a double life."

Eddie exhaled slowly and closed his eyes knowing that what was coming next would be nothing nice.

"Eddie, I'm HIV positive." The two men stare at each other for what seems like eons. All Eddie can think of is the status of his sister LaVerne.

"Does LaVerne…, is she ok?" Is the first question Karl hears.

"She's good, we haven't been intimate in three years. In fact, we've slept in separate rooms for the past two years." Eddie is surprised by this news. His sister never let on that on her home life was in shambles. *She's definitely Mattie's daughter* he says to himself.

"So how are you doing Karl? Is there anything I can do to help you out?"

"Actually Eddie, there is." Karl reaches into his jacket and pulls out a disc from the pocket. "I know this Sunday is third Sunday, so I want you to play this during the Church Family Meeting."

Eddie just stares at the disc for several long moments before looking back at Karl. "If my sister is ok with it, then yes."

"I've already spoken to LaVerne about it, and she supports me", Karl is quick to answer.

Knowing he doesn't have an out, Eddie nods his head as he reaches for the disc.

-CHAPTER 13-

"Ok, if that concludes all of the official church business, I'd like for everyone to pay attention to the screens", Reverend Eddie Majors Jr. instructs his flock as he points to the seventy foot projection screens that adorn the left and right sides of auditorium's front. "Brother Grady, lights please." A hush falls upon the congregation as the lights are dimmed.

"I know this is awkward, and very unconventional, but please listen very closely Brothers and Sisters. Sometime ago, I contracted HIV, and just recently it's developed into full-blown AIDS. Because I never got tested, the virus has done some pretty extensive damage to my body. I'm not sure how much longer I'll be with you, so there are some things I need to say.

First, to my wife, I'm sorry for all of the hurt and humiliation that I've brought into your life, and I pray that you find man who is worthy of you.

Secondly, to all of the men in here, if we've been together, it would be best if you get tested.

And finally to the women of this great church, I've had relations with quite a few of your husbands and boyfriends. For this, I am gravely sorry. Please, please, go and get tested…"

-CHAPTER 14-

He wonders how she'll react, what she'll say. They haven't seen each other in over twenty years. Edward Majors Jr. has flown to California to talk to his sisters. It's been a month since he discovered his childhood sweetheart, the girl he lost his virginity to, is actually his sister.

Eddie told no one of his travel plans. He grabbed the first flight departing from Metro Airport, and was on the left coast by nine a.m. pacific. The warmth of the Southern California sun did wonders for Eddie's psyche. It was November, and the drab grey and cold of Detroit had Eddie spiraling into a deep depression.

After leaving LAX, he has the taxi driver drop him off at Starbucks on Sepulveda, then sitting down to a Venti Pumpkin Spice Latte, Eddie decides to call Joan.

"Hello, may I speak with Joan please?"

"Who's this?" Joan inquires suspiciously, thinking him a bill collector.

"Joan, its Eddie", he says uneasily.

"Eddie Majors?"

"Yeah, it's me. How are you?"

"I'm good Eddie, how are you?"

"I'm pretty good, thanks."

"I'm sorry to hear about your dad. I know how close you were.

You know I understand, I had a hard time of it when Mom died", Joan says in a voice that's still tinged with the pain of loss.

"Yeah, whoever said that time heals all wounds, needs to let me kick them in the ass and start counting", Eddie says attempting to lighten the mood a bit. "How's your sister Joan?"

"Yolanda is doing well. She's practicing Corporate Law at one of the largest firms in Iowa. She's a real head-hunter, Acquisitions is her specialty. Hey, how's LaVerne?"

Eddie's mind flashes to the bedlam created by Karl's video before he answers. "Uh…she's fine. Listen Joan, I'm in town, and I was wondering if we could get together?"

"You're here?"

"Yeah, I'll be here until tomorrow morning, and I wanted to see you before I left." There is a pregnant pause before Joan answers.

"Uhh, I have a doctor's appointment at ten. Can we make it about noon?"

"Twelve is good, I'll meet you at Starbucks near LAX."

"Ok, see you then Eddie."

Nervous, Edward Majors Jr. hopes that his coming to LA isn't a giant mistake. What exactly he will say to Joan, he doesn't know. But, their sordid past has to be dealt with.

Joan was fifteen minutes late when she walked into the café. Eddie's breath caught as the adolescent feelings rushed in when he saw her. He felt like a degenerate as the images of their shared passion flashed in his mind.

"Hello Joan. Wow, it's been a lifetime since we've seen each other", he says as he stands to embrace her. "You look well. Time has been kind to you."

"Eddie, it's good to see you. What brings you out here?"

"Actually, you did."

"Me?" Joan asks as she takes a step backwards.

"Yeah, there's something we need to discuss. But before we get into that, let's go to a bar. I need something stronger than what Starbucks serves up."

"A bar, but aren't you a minister and all?"

"Yes, I am, but I still gets down. Remember, Jesus' first miracle was turning water into wine."

Twenty minutes later, Joan and Eddie are seated in a dark hotel bar. "Ok Eddie, what's up?"

"Joan, this is awkward as hell for me, so I'll just come out with it. I just recently found out that Uncle Ellis.., er your dad, is actually my father. He and my mother had an affair, and I'm the product of it." Eddie brings his glass to his mouth and gulps down its fiery contents. He looks at Joan to see if she realizes the implications of his statement. What he sees puzzles him.

"Eddie, I know."

"You know? Damn! So I'm the last to know. What kinda shit is that? So, how long have you known?

"Eddie, I found out right before we moved here. My father, our father decided to come clean when he discovered you and I had…you know", Joan said averting her eyes.

"So, is that why you all moved so suddenly?"

"Yes, that's one of the reasons", Joan says.

"I always suspected that, but was never sure."

"So does Yolanda know?" Eddie asks.

"Yeah, she knows. That's the reason she ended up in Iowa. She said she couldn't deal with all of the mess that was in our home."

"Wait a sec, you said that was one of the reasons, what else don't I know?"

"Eddie, I was pregnant when we moved out here…."

-CHAPTER 15-

Eddie returns from the bathroom only after splashing his face with cold water, and cleaning his left shoe. The force of the involuntary vomiting had his stomach muscles twisted in a knot.

Joan is standing at the entrance of the bar with a worried look about her. Eddie pays their tab, and gives the barmaid a healthy tip for what he left on the floor.

"Are you ok Eddie?"

"Hell no! I just never imagined that my life would take the drastic turns it has. I don't even know who I am anymore…"

"I know this is a lot to have to digest in such a short period."

"So how is the baby, is it normal?" Eddie couldn't bring himself to say *our baby*.

"Our daughter Heather was born healthy, thank God. My folks flew me back to Detroit to stay with my Uncle Tillman and Aunt Bertha when I got to my third trimester, because they didn't want the church to know about my sin."

"Wait a minute, so you had the baby in Detroit?"

"Yeah, I was at Grace Hospital. Is it true they closed it down?"

"Yes, Grace Hospital closed there on Meyers and 7 mile, and then merged with Sinai Hospital. So the old Mount Carmel is now Sinai Grace."

"That's fitting Eddie, even the place where our daughter was born is only a memory", Joan says with much pain.

Eddie embraces Joan and they hold each other in silence for several moments.

"Joan, I'm so sorry you've had to endure this alone for all of these years. I had no idea."

"I know, I was so messed up when I found out that I was carrying my brother's baby that I almost cracked up."

"When did you find out Joan?"

"My parents convinced me that I had to give Heather up for adoption. So when I was filing the necessary documents, our father decided it was time to 'fess up. Needless to say, after years of strong meds and psychiatric care, I'm able to function."

"So, do you know who adopted her?"

"The only thing I know is that it was an older couple who lived on the Westside at the time."

"I know a very good private detective Joan, I'll find her."

"Eddie, are you sure you want to get into this?"

"Joan, I have a daughter out there somewhere, I have to find her."

-CHAPTER 16-

Reverend Edward Majors Jr. maneuvered through the always under construction Eastbound I-94. As soon as his plane touched down, Eddie knew exactly what he was to do.

The first call he placed was to his accountant Lee Goldenberg. After that, Hubert Heath of *Eagle Eye Private Detectives*, who Eddie kept on retainer was roused and given a new assignment.

Next, Dara Baldwin, Eddie's lawyer, was receiving his call.

"Hello Reverend Majors, how are you these days? I haven't spoken to you since your father's memorial service. Ok, are you sure? Wow, well in that case, since you want the best, I suggest you go with *Maxine and Roi*. They're the absolute best in the Metro Area. Certainly Eddie and I wish you the best."

Eddie needs something to calm his nerves before he makes the next calls on his list, so he searches his CD changer until he finds Smooth Jazz artist *Tim Reeves'* disc.

"Hey Rita. Yeah, I know, I know. I had some really important business I had to deal with. Look, why don't you call and make us a reservation at your favorite spot for dinner. That's fine; I'll meet you there at seven."

Eddie's final call is the most important one. "Hey baby, how are you? Calm down for a second dammit! Look, I'll be by about 9:30, we have a lot to talk about. I really can't get into it right now Loretta. Why do you always go there with me? Not now, shit!"

Eddie taps his Bluetooth earpiece and ends the call.

Eddie has had a very nagging feeling every since he got on his return flight to Detroit. He prayed silently that his suspicions were way off base. Not being able to contain himself any longer, Eddie dials Marc-Anthony's number. As usual, Eddie is sent to voicemail.

"Marc-Anthony, I really need to speak with you this evening, call me back ASAP."

"Damn why is he always hitting me up when I'm wit you?" Marc-Anthony asks Heather as they walk into his bedroom.

"I don't know, but he be trippin' me out the way he's always lookin' at me like he know me from somewhere but can't remember where.

"He had the nerve to try and get in my shit after my GrandPa's funeral about me and you."

"For real, what he say?"

"Some shit about be careful what and who I do."

-CHAPTER 17-

"Eddie, I'm so glad you wanted to come here, you know how much I love *Sinbad's*!"

"I know Rita, and I thought it only fitting that our last meal together as Mr. and Mrs. Edward Majors Jr. be here."

Rita nearly chokes on her *Grand Marnier, Remy Martin* and *Coke*. "Excuse me?! Oh hell naw! I know you ain't tryna play me likes this!"

"Rita c'mon, let's not make a scene, let's be adults about it."

"*Adults* my ass! You can't divorce me, you'll lose everything. You think I don't know about you and Loretta?"

"Rita, I'm sorry, I never wanted to hurt you, but you and I both know that the thrill has been gone for a long time."

"So what, you think I'mma let you just kick me to the curb, and give that bitch my spot? Nigga, fuck you wit a sick dick!"

Eddie laments over the hand he's being forced to play, but knowing what his soon to be ex-wife is like, he's prepared for this day.

"Rita, I really didn't want to ever have to go here with you. But, since you've left me with no choice, I'll leave you with no voice...." Eddie reaches inside his blazer, and removes an envelope. He ceremoniously slides the envelope across the table to Rita. Rita Renelle Majors removes the twenty vivid color photos of her and Deacon Horton in various compromising positions of congress.

"It would appear that we are at an impasse Rita. Now we can get all messy and go through a nasty divorce, or we can both own up to what we've done, and be amicable about this."

Seeing that Rita was still flipping through the *Days of Her Life*, Eddie decided to proceed.

"Of course, the house is yours. And I'm relinquishing myself of all rights and matters of Faith Fellowship Christian Church, and signing them over to you, which is more than generous on my part, because I could easily just sign my fifty percent over to LaVerne, and be done with it. But I'm not that kind of man. Besides, you've given me two wonderful sons. Now all of this is of course is contingent on you just letting me walk," Eddie says as he stands and drops some money on the table for the meal.

-CHAPTER 18-

Loretta opens the door and just turns her back to Eddie as he enters. Loretta is marching purposefully to her den, where she plans on making her stand. She sits down on the couch and gets comfortable before the blasting is to start.

"I'm divorcing Rita", Eddie says suddenly before her eruption can begin.

"What?"

"I'm divorcing Rita I said. I just told her that I was done."

Loretta's eyelids flutter like hummingbird wings. Her mouth opens and closes several times before she can speak.

"Eddie, you don't know how long I've dreamed of you saying those exact words. Please tell me you're serious."

Eddie walks over to Loretta and kneels in front of her. "Baby, today I realized that you're the only real thing in my life. I knew that I loved you, but I always put the family's affairs ahead of my needs. Loretta, I want nothing more than to be able to live and love with you for as long as life will allow us."

"But what about the church?"

"I'm walking away from it totally. I can't deal anymore. Since my Dad died, I've found out some very disturbing things, and I need time to deal with them properly. I'm a very fragmented person right now, and hurt people, hurt people. We'll be good, I've got some money put away."

Eddie sits next to Loretta and he tells of his secret identity, and the sordid details of him and Joan.

"So what are you going to do about your daughter Eddie?"

"I've got a Private Detective on the case. He's quite thorough, so I should know something within the next few days or so."

Eddie's phone vibrates with a call suddenly. "Mr. Majors?"

"Yes Hubert, what have you got for me?"

"Well I found her, and you're not gonna believe this, but she's been right up under your nose…"

CHAPTER 19

"What the hell!?" Marc-Anthony yells as he's startled by his father bursting into his room. "What are you doing?"

"Heather, please get your clothes on and wait for me in the library."

"Pastor Eddie it's not what you think…"

"Heather, the library please", Eddie says as he turns around to allow her some privacy. After she leaves, Eddie closes the bedroom door, and slides down the wall to the floor.

"Dad, you didn't have to blow up my spot like that! I was gonna return your call in a minute!"

"Marc-Anthony, please tell me you use a condom…"

"Of course! I ain't trying to seminate none of these hoes", Marc-Anthony says with ghetto bravado.

"That *hoe* you've just referred to is actually your half-sister son."

"Ok, I know you've been trippin' about her since the funeral, but you don't have to come at me with some sideways crap like that Pops."

"I wish it wasn't the case, but I just found out that I fathered Heather with my first girlfriend, so you've been sleeping with your half-sister Marc-Anthony." Eddie's son searches his face for some sign of trickery.

"Well why didn't you just tell me instead of sweating me all the time about her?"

"I didn't even know about Heather until today. It was always something familiar about her to me, but I could never figure out what."

"You gon' hafta tell her, cuz I can't deal with this."

"Don't worry, I'll break the news to her Marc-Anthony, we'll get through this together."

-CHAPTER 20-

Faith Fellowship Christian Church is filled to capacity for the monthly Church Family Meeting. Pastor Eddie made it known that today's meeting affected every member of the church.

"I want to thank each and every one of you for being in attendance this afternoon. The reason I've asked you all to be here today, is to let you know that as of this moment, I will no longer be your leader." Eddie allows the shocked congregation to settle down before he continues.

"I feel it's only right that I confess to you, my brothers and sisters that I am not the man you think me to be. I am not the seed of the man who graced this podium prior to me. Because of the choices that he and my biological father, Reverend Ellis Perry made I unwittingly impregnated my sister who was also not aware of our relation.

Mother Tolbert's top row of dentures fell out of her mouth in her surprise. Eddie scanned the shell-shocked auditorium and forged ahead.

"Ironically, as the Good Lord would have it, my daughter has come to be a member here. You all know Sister Heather over there", Eddie says pointing to her.

By this point, the attendees are flabbergasted, and realize that there is more to come as Pastor Eddie raises his hands to shush everyone.

"I am also divorcing my wife of 25 years, so that I may spend my remaining years with the woman that has had my heart for at least a decade. Loretta Roberts and I are resigning together in fact." Eddie is somewhat surprised by the lack of shocked expressions in the crowd.

"Rita Majors will be assuming my position as head of the Executive Board, and will be choosing the next pastor of this great church immediately."

Edward Majors Jr. looks around the vast expanse of faces, and tries to make eye contact with as many as he can. His eyes well up with tears as he takes in the beauty of the church from his perspective one final time.

"So as you can see, I am not the man you thought I was. I'm not even the man I thought I was. I'm a man with far ranging and deeply personal issues. So as I leave here today not exactly knowing what my future holds, I leave here knowing this one thing, that I am just a man."

Judgment Day

By: Rebecca Striggles

-Chapter 1-

It is a beautiful Spring Sunday afternoon, and service has just ended, people are standing around socializing in their Sunday's best. Many stand in line to have their turn to shake hands with Pastor Young to tell him how anointed his sermon was.

To me, Pastor Young is just another hypocritical, scandalous, money hungry, adulterer, but we'll get back to that later. I'm sure you are wondering why I attend his church if I think he is so horrible. It's because I don't have a choice. My dad is an Associate Minister, my mom is an Evangelist, and my boyfriend is a Deacon in Training. Not to mention, my sisters sing in the choir, and my brother is the Minister of Music.

As for me I used to help out with the Children's Ministry, but I gave that up a few months ago. There will be too many questions that I don't want to answer if I were to leave this church. The *Word* that Pastor Young preaches is so good, why would I want to leave?

Today turned out to be a really beautiful day. The sun is out, there are very few clouds and there is a nice breeze blowing. I'm standing near a tree waiting for my boyfriend Aaron to get done kissing Pastor Young's ass so we can go eat.

Aaron is smart young man; I don't understand why he can't see straight through Pastor Young's fake ass. As I'm standing here watching Aaron, I'm realizing how truly fine he is. His tall, well-built frame is enough to turn any woman on. He has a six-pack that's out of this world! Sometimes I fantasize about us fucking. Yes, I said *fantasize*. We've been together now for five years and have not had sex.

Aaron wants to wait until we marry. This is twisted! The man is holding out on the woman! When our wedding night comes, if this nigga's dick game ain't good, I'm getting an annulment!

"Arian, why are you standing here alone with your fine *you know what*?" That's Dorian, Aaron's best friend interrupting my thoughts.

"Hey Dorian, how are you?"

"Not as fine as you look, but I know what you can do to make me that way."

"Dorian, you need to stop. You couldn't get any of this if you were the last man on earth. And if you were, you wouldn't be able to handle it. Besides, you know I'm saving my body, my *Temple of the Lord*, for when Aaron becomes my husband."

"Girl, you can drop the innocent act. You might be able to fool these church people, but you can't fool me. I see right through you. I know you want it just as bad as I do. I see it in your eyes, for you to be all saved and holy, you sure look at me lustfully. Anyway, I don't know what you're doing with that fool anyhow. If he were half the man I am, he would be hittin' that every chance he gets.

Because if it were me, my dick and your pussy would be magnetized every time we were alone."

Laughing, I replied, "Boy you know I'm saved, and I don't fornicate. And I think this conversation is a little inappropriate to be having in front of the house of God."

"Quit frontin'! I know you want me. I know you want to feel my long, hard dick in you."

"In your dreams Dorian!" In the back of my mind I was wondering how he could see through me so easily. Dorian is fine, with his smooth high yellow skin complexion; tall, slender frame perfectly tapered straight hair and full mustache and goatee to match. If he wasn't Aaron's best friend, I'd fuck him. And he's looking real fuckable today in his dark blue single-breasted suit with a cream shirt and tie along with cream and blue gators. I wonder what size shoe he wears? Because brother gots some big feet, and you know what the say about men with big feet.

Before Dorian had time to reply to my last comment Aaron walked up, so we had to end out little chit-chat.

"Hey sweetie," I said. "You ready to go eat?"

"Yes, but don't you want to go speak to Pastor Young first? I was just talking to him and he had some very nice and encouraging things to say about us. He also mentioned that the two of you haven't talked in quite a while now."

Damn! I thought to myself. I needed to come up with an excuse and I can't think of anything! Dorian, who was still standing there, saw the uneasiness on my face and bailed me out.

"Man, Arian was just telling me how hungry she is. Y'all better get a move on before all the restaurants get crowded and you end up being late for evening service. I know how you hate to be late, and not be able to sit on the front row. She can talk to Pastor Young after evening service."

"Ok." Aaron replied. "I'm quite hungry myself. Arian what do you want to eat?"

"I have a taste for Catfish with some Macaroni and Cheese and Candied Yams."

"You ain't tired of eating *Irene's Southern Cooking* yet? Seems like you go there every week" Dorian says.

Aaron invites Dorian to come with us. I hate being with the two of them at the same time because Dorian makes sexual advances toward me when Aaron isn't paying attention. Not that I don't like the gestures and attention, I just feel bad that he's doing this behind Aaron's back. Since Dorian is coming, I suggested that we invite my friend Elise to come along also. I tell Aaron and Dorian to wait in the car while I go to find Elise.

-Chapter 2-

I go straight to our usual hangout spot in the church basement to find Elise, but she isn't there. No one in the room knows where she is. I check all of the ladies' rooms, no Elise. Then I bump into my dumb ass sister Alicia.

"Alicia have you seen Lise?"

"I saw her go into Conference Room B with Deacon Anderson about fifteen minutes ago."

Something about that just didn't sit right with me, but I ignored it until I reached Conference Room B. The door is closed, but I can hear some rather loud whispers. I open the door to find Deacon Anderson holding Elise by her arms, shaking her.

"Look you little ho, you will not…" He stops talking mid-sentence when he notices me standing in the doorway.

"Get your hands off her!" I yell. We stare each other down.

"Now!!" I yell even louder. Elise has a look of sadness and distress on her face, and she's trying hard not to cry.

"Lise, are you ok, did he hurt you?" I ask.

"She is fine…I would never hurt Sister Elise." Deacon Anderson says defensively.

"I believe I was talking to her. And by the way you were grabbing her didn't exactly look like you were *touching and agreeing* on something together."

"We were just talking."

"I believe God blessed her with a voice and a mouth to go along with it. So why don't you shut yours and let her speak for herself?"

It may seem like I'm disrespecting this *Man of God*, but knowing what I know, and what I've experienced, something horrific has happened.

"Lise, what's going on here?" Instead of responding Elise just runs past me to the ladies room down the hall. Deacon Anderson and I stare at each other for a moment.

"Yea, she seems just fine to me." I finally say.

"Pray for her, the Holy Spirit is dealing with her."

I can't believe this fool said that! I go to the ladies room to comfort Elise, and to find out what that asshole had done to her. As I enter, Elise is coming out of one of the stalls. Her face, beet red and wet with tears.

"What's going on?!" I ask as Elise begins to sob again. It breaks my heart to see her like this. All I can do is hug her and let her know that I am here for her. Finally, Elise is able to compose herself.

"I'll be fine Arian, don't worry about me, I'm just under a lot of stress right now, and I don't want to talk about it."

"Whenever you're ready to talk, you know I'm here for you." It's tearing me up inside to see her like this. I want to kick Deacon Anderson's ass for whatever it is he did to her.

"Let's go, Aaron and Dorian is waiting for us in the car, we're going to *Irene's*."

-Chapter 3-

Once we get to *Irene's* I'm not surprised to see so many familiar faces from our church and other churches that we fellowship with. However, I am surprised to see this one bitch named Nicole.

We went to high school together; she hates me because she wants Aaron. She spread some pretty vicious lies about me, made people turn on me, and bullshit like that. Now here we are three years later, and this bitch has two little ones that look just like her. And she looks like she will explode any day now with another one.

What a ho! I bet she doesn't even know who their fathers are. She sure wanted Aaron to be one. Right now I wish I had a camera to catch the expression on her face when she sees that Aaron and I are still together. This ho tried every trick in the book to break us up. Once, it worked, but not for long. We were back together within a month.

Nicole comes over to us, and gives Aaron a big hug. She barely acknowledges me of course.

"How are you these days Aaron?"

"Things are great! What about you?"

She tells him she's due any day, and that they should keep in touch. By this time the hostess is calling us to be seated. This was perfect timing because if she had touched Aaron's face one more time, I would have slapped the shit out of her.

Dorian, who noticed that I was annoyed, tries to distract me and guide me to our table as we follow the hostess. As he's pulling me along, I look back and notice Aaron is all in Nicole's ugly ass face. What's being said, I don't know, but his body language looks angry and hostile. Not knowing what that was about, when Aaron gets to the table, I ask him.

"It's nothing Arian, I was just telling her not to be so disrespectful towards you." I don't really buy it, but I'll let it go for now. "I'm so hungry, and it smells so good in here!" Elise says. She's come back to herself, finally.

"Me too Lise, I'm having my usual."

"I think I'm going to have Turkey and Dressing, with sides of Greens and Mac and Cheese," she replies.

"I could go for some Fried Pork Chops," Dorian says.

"Babe, what are you having?" I ask Aaron.

"I'm not hungry anymore."

"On the way here you were saying how you couldn't wait to get here to eat, and now you're not hungry?

"I'm not feeling well; I guess I lost my appetite."

I'm a firm believer in Women's Intuition, and mine is telling me that he didn't suddenly become ill. That nasty, trifling, ho ass bitch Nicole has something to do with this. His whole mood has changed, especially after the heated exchange between him and that heifer.

"We can get our food to go; do you want to go home?"

"No I'll be fine."

"You should go home and get some rest. Skip evening service so you can get better."

"I'm fine! I just don't feel like eating right now Arian. Stop being so pushy!" He snaps at me.

He better be glad that today is Sunday and we just left church, otherwise I'd be cussing him out right now. That nigga knows better than to talk to me like that!! I am so shocked by his behavior.

Even Dorian and Lise were surprised. He never acts this way. I know one thing, this bullshit better not ever happen again. And, I'm going to get to the bottom of whatever this thing is he has with Nicole.

-Chapter 4-

Alicia and Adrian, my two sisters, walk over to our table to say speak. I knew when I saw Alicia's bitch ass earlier she looked strange. Now I know why. It's because she's wearing my $400 *Prada* shoes and the $ 600 matching purse, along with a pair of my *Dolce* and *Gabanna* sunglasses. I should beat her ass all over this restaurant!

"Alicia sweetheart, why are you wearing my things?" I manage to say through gritted teeth.

"Arian, why are you so stingy? It ain't like this stuff is real anyway.

Did this bitch just say that?

"I know that the money Mom and Dad gives you isn't enough for you to buy the real thing." Well, homegirl managed to get one thing right, the money my folks give me is not enough to support my expensive tastes. But she got it all twisted, ain't none of my shit fake!

"All I know is all my stuff better be back where it belongs tonight, and if anything else is missing, you'll be very sorry."

"Whatever! You stingy ho!"

I don't have a job because I'm a full-time college student. My parents don't want me to work because they want me to put all of my focus and energy into school. They want me to be a successful lawyer, so every week Daddy gives me $200 to spend as I please. The thing that no one but Elise, Pastor Young and I know is that

Pastor Young tosses me a grand every week, to keep our little secret.

I know you want to know what that secret is, but I'm still not ready to discuss it yet.

-Chapter 5-

On the way back to church, Aaron was completely silent. I could tell he was lost in thought and that something was deeply troubling him. I didn't press the issue though. If he snaps at me again like he did at the restaurant, I won't be as nice.

Evening service was ok, I was glad when it ended so I could go home. On my way out, I tried to avoid Aaron and Pastor Young. Just when I thought I was home free, I heard the raspy voice of Pastor Young. I tried pretending that I didn't hear him, but it didn't work, because Aaron started calling me also. I stopped walking, and turning around, I pasted on the best smile that could.

"Praise the Lord Sister Arian, it's so good to see you. You look like God has been blessing you."

"He has." I dryly responded.

"How is school?"

"Fine."

"I know God is blessing you with straight A's."

"Yup."

"Aaron, she's not very talkative tonight is she?"

"She must still be caught up in the Spirit Pastor." My ass-kissing boyfriend said.

"Well, you take care now, and be a blessing to someone else's life so that God will continue to bless you. I'm going to go lay hands on Sister Thomas, she's not feeling well."

"Ok," I said.

When Pastor Young walked away Aaron looked as if he wanted to strangle me.

"Arian, why are you acting like that? Is it because of what happened at the restaurant? If you got beef with me, take it out on me, not other people. The way you acted towards Pastor Young was completely uncalled for. You owe him an apology. As a matter of fact you owe me one too. You completely embarrassed me!" He bitched.

"Aaron calm down! You wanted me to talk to Pastor Young and I did! I don't see what the problem is."

"You were rude to him. You can't treat the Man of God like that. He told me earlier today that he has a prophecy for us, and he wants to share it with both of us at the same time. Now because of the way you acted he may not share it with us."

"If he received a Word from God for us... if he's a true Man of God, he would tell us no matter what."

"Maybe God told him not to because of the way you acted!"

"You sound so ridiculous, and Aaron, you got one more time to raise your voice at me!"

"Arian I'm so disgusted with you right now. You need to get a ride home with one of your sisters because I'm so furious with you right now, I don't even want to look at you."

Aaron stormed off and left me in the sanctuary all alone. I'm glad no else was in there to witness our argument. Aaron better be glad that we were in church; otherwise he would have gotten cussed out. I had to go find one of my dumb ass sisters before they left.

As I went to the basement, I wondered why Aaron had his head stuck so far up Young's ass. Why can't he see him for the fraud that he is? How come he couldn't see how Pastor Young was eye-fucking me the whole time he was talking to me?

Just as I turned the corner to enter the dining hall, I bumped right into Dorian.

"Girl you better watch where you're going."

"Sorry Dorian. Have you seen any of my sisters?"

"They all just left."

"Damn! Oops, I mean *darn*."

"Ha!" Dorian said as he formed one of those sexy ass grins.

"You don't have to front with me Arian. I know you have to with everyone else, but not with me. I want you to be you. That is the only way you can be happy. You can't keep pretending to be someone you aren't. I like the real you. I think you have a freaky, bad girl side, and it turns me on."

"Whatever Dorian, I need a ride home. Do you mind taking me?"

"Where's Aaron?"

"He got mad at me, and told me to find another way home."

"He just left you without making sure had a way first?"

"Yup."

"That's cold, what if nobody was here? Your family is already gone, what if I wasn't here?"

"Then I'd have to call somebody to come back and get me."

"He shouldn't have left you like that."

"It's been a long day. Will you just take me home please Dorian?"

"I'd love to take you to my crib. I can think of a few things I could do to help you unwind."

"Maybe I better call one of my sisters to come get me. You might try to take me back to your place, and fulfill all of your little nasty fantasies." I teased.

"I promise I won't try anything. I wouldn't enjoy it, if you weren't enjoying it. When it *does* go down between us, you're gonna be wishing that you didn't wait so long. *And* I won't tell Aaron."

"There won't be anything for you to tell Aaron. Why can't you get it through your head that nothing is going to happen with us? I love Aaron, and will never cheat on him, especially with you."

"What are you so scared of? I know you are curious, and I'm almost positive you're not a virgin. I'm offering to step up to the plate, and pick up where Aaron is slacking."

"I don't need your volunteer services. And how are you gonna assume that I'm not a virgin?"

"Because of the way you're shaped, and the way you carry yourself. Your hips are shaped like somebody has been between them. You're not naive like most of these church girls. I can tell they're virgins."

"Whatever Dorian, will you just take me home please?"

On the way home, I realized that I didn't have any cash, and I wouldn't have time to stop at the ATM before class in the morning. Fuck! I didn't want to spend a minute longer than I had to in the car with Dorian.

"Dorian, would it be too much trouble for you to stop at a *Comerica* for me?"

"Of course not." Dorian pulled up to the ATM machine, and that was when I realized that I would have to lean across him to do my transaction. He must have realized it too, because he had a sly grin on his face.

Then it hit me, I could just get out the car and do it.

Just when I was about to open the door, Dorian grabbed my arm and asked, "Are you sure you want to do that?"

"Why wouldn't I?"

"Because it is pouring rain." He was right; I had been so lost in my thoughts about us having sex, that I hadn't even noticed the rain. I'm a black girl, with black girl hair. Moisture and my hair don't get along well. Dorian and I exchanged a long stare.

"Arian, I'm not going to bite you, unless you want me to. You might be kinky like that. I'm down for whatever."

"Could you at least recline your seat so I can get out the window?"

"No problem."

I put my card in the machine, and did what I had to do. It seemed as if the machine was taking an extra long time to process my transaction. Maybe it's the intense gaze that Dorian was giving me that had me buggin."

After I collected my cash and card from the machine, and was coming back through the window, Dorian surprised me by kissing me on my neck. I turned towards him, and was about to let him have it, but before I could get a word out he gently kissed me on the lips. The touch from his lips sent a chill through my body. All I could do was stare in his eyes, speechless.

"I'm so sorry Arian, I don't know what got into me, I'm completely out of line. I know I talk a lot of shit, but I had no intentions of doing anything. I don't know what came over me." I just stared at him still speechless. "Say something Arian. I'm so sorry."

Before he could say anything else, I found myself kissing him. I held his face in my hands, and he wrapped his arms around my waist. Then his hands moved from my waist to my ass. Mine moved from his face, to his chest. Then one of his hands found its way to my breast, and began to gently caress it.

Dorian pushed me over into my seat, and reclined it, then he moved over on top of me. His hands were everywhere now, rubbing, squeezing, caressing, massaging and I liked it. He started moving his hand under my skirt, and up my thigh. I let out a slight moan. It'd been so long since I'd been touched like that. As he moved his way up my thigh, he stopped kissing me, and stared deeply into my eyes. Our eyes locked for a few moments. The look in his eyes really turned me on. It was a deep and intense longing. I could see how badly he wanted me.

It felt so good to be desired like that. Just when his hand was reaching that *special place*, my cell phone rang. *FUCK! FUCK! FUCK!* I decided to ignore it, but Dorian insisted I answer it, and wouldn't you know its Aaron.

"Hey Babe, just checking to see if you made it home ok, and to apologize for the way I acted. I'm really sorry. I overreacted, and I was a real jerk at the restaurant."

"Ok. I have to go."

"What are you doing?"

"My phone is breaking up. I'll call you back."

"Where are you?"

"Hello? Hello? I can't hear you. I'll call you in the morning. Love you, bye."

I hung up the phone, and turned to Dorian, who was staring out the window.

"I'm taking you home now."

"Ok Dorian." What I really wanted to say was, *The hell you are! You're gonna take me back to your place and beat my pussy up!*

"What are you going to tell Aaron?"

"Nothing. What are you going to tell Aaron?"

"Not a damn thing."

-Chapter 6-

WHAT THE FUCK?!! I can't believe this!!!! While I was in class, Aaron accidentally called my phone. There's a three minute long message of him telling that bitch Nicole that neither of her babies are his, and having sex with her was a mistake. That trashy bitch is telling him that my pussy will never be as good as hers, even though I'm a virgin. Also, that she's about to take him to Court for Child Support.

Aaron replies by saying he wants a Paternity Test. That bitch needs to stop talking about my pussy! Little does she know, I'm not a virgin. My pussy is so good; my bills get paid every month. Oops! Did I let that slip out? I'm still not ready to discuss it yet.

Oh God! I think I'm gonna cry. How could Aaron do this to me?! As good to him as I've been, as patient as I've been!! How could he?! This really confirms my theory that niggas ain't shit!!!! Aaron's fucked around on the wrong one, and I'mma make sure he regrets it.

I can't believe I actually thought that a nigga as fine as him, at his age is still a virgin. I've been so stupid!!!! I need a drink like a muthafucka!!

-Chapter 7-

After class I went home and took a nap. The unexpected discovery exhausted me. I needed to recuperate. The strangest thing happened during my nap, I had an erotic dream about Dorian. Just thinking about it again makes my panties wet.

I'm startled out of my thoughts about that sexy ass nigga by my ringing telephone. "Hello?"

"Girl, can you come over? I need to talk." This is Elise, sounding on the verge of tears.

"I'm on my way." I state and hang up the phone immediately. Twenty minutes later, I'm seated on a couch at Elise's, and can't believe the bullshit that she's telling.

Here is the gist of the story. One Friday night, Elise went to a bar alone to have a drink. Well, she ends up having more than one and runs into Deacon Anderson when she finally decided to leave the bar. They were both equally surprised to see each other there. Deacon Anderson insisted on buying Elise a drink. Apparently, they both had one too many drinks and ended up at the *Hillside Hotel.*

The next morning, they both agreed to never speak on it again. Deacon Anderson and Elise both kept their word, and acted as if they didn't do all the nasty, freaky things that Elise said they did. I wish she had spared me the details. He's not my cup of tea, and damn sure wouldn't fit into any of my sexual fantasies. I can think of someone else who will though. Let me get back to the story before I get all hot and bothered.

As I was saying, neither of them acted as if anything had happened, that was until Elise realized that she's pregnant. She had just told him on Sunday, when I walked in on them.

"He wants me to get and abortion, said he'll pay for it."

"So… let him." I offer.

"I know I probably should, but I don't think that I can live with myself if I kill this innocent baby."

"So, keep it."

"He said he'll kill me if I don't get rid of it. I know it sounds ridiculous, but I believe he will. You know two of his sons are Hitmen, all he has to do is say the word and I'm done. Then he'll be at my funeral giving remarks on behalf of the Deacon's Board. Talking about how God works in mysterious ways, and how He wanted me in Heaven with Him because I'm so special."

"Elise honey, that man is not going to have you killed, and He'll be sorry for threatening you. As a matter of fact, we're going to make a couple of people live with regret."

"What are you talking about Arian?

"I've been played for a damn fool big time."

"Aren't you supposed to be here for me helping me with my problem, how'd we end up on yours? You still haven't told me what I should do about this baby. I for damn sure, don't want to be pregnant. Do you know how nasty I might look?

"Elise, quit trippin'."

"Any man that says a pregnant woman is the most beautiful thing they've seen is a motherfucking liar Arian! With her nose stretched twice as wide as it already is, not to mention the fucked up attitudes pregnant women have.

"True."

"I'm already a bitch naturally; can you imagine how I will be when I'm eight months pregnant?

I don't want to imagine it.

"On top of all that, you can't fuck! If you can at the end of your pregnancy it's probably not good, and then you can't for almost two months after. I love to fuck! I haven't gone that long without fucking since I've been fucking!!"

"Girl you are so crazy," I say laughing. "I can't make up your mind for you, but whatever you do; I'll support you one hundred percent. Now you know that I am self-absorbed, so with that being said, can we get back to my drama?"

"Go on girl, I know you're dying to let it out."

"Aaron has been fucking that bitch Nicole." I state calmly for dramatic effect.

"Get the fuck out of here! No way! Not that ugly bitch! Aaron can't be that dumb! You must be mistaken."

I just sit there and give her a look.

"How can you be so sure?" she questions.

"Because, while I was at school today he accidentally called me and I sent him straight to voicemail. When I got out of class I listened to my messages, and when I got to his, he was having a heart-to-heart with that bitch! Telling her how neither one of those babies are his. She was telling him that my pussy can't compare to hers, and that he needs to leave me so that they can be the family that they should be."

"Girl, shut up!" Elise exclaims.

"At the end of the message, he told her that this would be their last time fucking, and that he don't want to see her anymore. I must have listened to that message fifteen times before I heard the whole thing. It's like I would listen to a little bit of it, and then become so furious that I didn't hear the rest of it."

"So what's your devious plan for revenge?"

"I have no idea. I knew some shit was up though after I saw how they acted when we were at *Irene's*. I knew it would just be a matter of time before it fell into my lap like everything else does. I wanted to believe Aaron has better sense than this."

"Arian he must be thinking with the wrong head."

"Alicia is getting the whole scoop for me, she still fucks Pastor Evan's son Maurice, and he goes with Nicole's sister Natalie. That is one thing I can say about my sisters, even though we can't stand each other, we always have each other's back in the time of need."

Suddenly, my cell phone rings. "Speak of the devil! What's up Alicia?"

"Well, I just left Maurice's apartment."

"Were you able to find out anything?"

"Was I!? At first he didn't want to talk, but once I started giving him some first-class head, he started singing like a canary."

"Please spare me the details of the *blow by blow*, tell me what I need to know."

Elise sat waiting patiently for me to get off the phone. Alicia and I finally hung up, and I had to sit for a few seconds in silence to digest what I just heard.

"The start of this little affair or whatever you want to call it is the most... I'm at a loss of words Elise, for the first time ever."

"Just tell me what was said." Elise says as she passes me the Hard Lemonade that she got from the kitchen while I was on the phone. She knew I'd need it to calm my nerves.

"That dumb fuck Aaron couldn't even fuck, and still ended up with a baby."

"What? You lost me already Arian."

"Aaron's brother Ira was trying to fuck Nicole's girl Denise, so he invites her over when their parents were out of town. Denise brought Nicole along with her, and Ira had Aaron entertain Nicole. Apparently, he tried to fuck her, but couldn't keep his pathetic worm of a dick up. However, he did manage to get some pre-nut in her, and that's how she got pregnant."

"That is so sad girl! I have two questions for you though, how is she claiming that baby number two is his if they didn't really fuck? Secondly, why did you describe his dick as a worm?"

"After he found out that she was pregnant they started fucking for real. I guess he decided what good is having a baby if you didn't have fun making it? His dick is a worm, because it for damn sure ain't an anaconda."

"Wow, that's deep. We both have some drama right now. It must be handled with care."

Elise ain't said but a word. This shit will most definitely be handled with care.

-Chapter 8-

Alicia called Aaron for me telling him I had a bad case of sinusitis and lost my voice. This bought me some time, and excused me from having to speak to Aaron on the phone. I'm not very good at hiding my emotions. I would need a couple of days away from Aaron to be able to get to the point where I could act as if everything was normal. I just hope that he doesn't come to see me.

Elise and I formulated a plan of action for dealing with Deacon Anderson over breakfast this morning. I'm still trying to figure out how to deal with Aaron. After breakfast with 'Lise, I headed to the mall to do my favorite thing, and get a massage. As I was walking through a store I bump into Pastor Young, one of the last people I wished to see.

Hey baby is how he greets me.

"Hello Pastor Young."

"Arian don't talk to me like that. You know we're better than this. When are we gon' hook up again so that we can get to know each other even better."

"Never, Pastor Young."

"You know Arian, I was thinking about our situation the other day. I asked myself why am I still paying you and I ain't getting no pussy? I've come to the conclusion that I have paid more than enough over the years, and I'm done now. If you're not going to give me any of that sweet ass pussy anymore, why should I continue to pay you?"

"It's simple, you owe me. You need to be paying me for the rest of my life for what you put me through."

"Don't act like you didn't like it, I know I gots good dick."

"What about how you raped me, and manipulated me into thinking that that's what God wanted? What about how you forced me to have an abortion, and convinced me that God told you it was ok?"

"That, my dear, is called *Game*. You didn't have to continue fucking me after all that, but you wanted to, because you liked it, and I bet you still do. Let's go get a room now."

"I was only thirteen when you did that horrible stuff to me. I believed that no Man of God would do anything wrong. After all, you are the Pastor; God should talk to you the most. You will never get near this pussy again. Do you know how traumatized I was? I started sneaking and going to meetings for Rape Victims, that's how I realized what you did was completely wrong."

"Arian, that's in the past now, I have apologized to you over and over again. Now you need to let it go. The Bible says to forgive those that have done you wrong, so forgive me. You must have already; otherwise you wouldn't have continued having sex with me. I'm going over to the hotel and get a room. Arian, if you want to continue receiving your checks, then you'll come to the room with me today, and any other day that I want to see you."

"You will never get that nasty ass dick of yours anywhere near me again. And, I'm going to continue getting my check every week. As a matter of fact I want a raise. The price of living is increasing and my pay should too."

"Ha! Little bitch, you have lost your mind!"

"No, but I think you have. Have you forgotten about the night I went to our room and caught you and Elder Duncan screwing?"

"Look Arian, bottom line, I'm not paying you another red cent unless I'm getting my dick sucked and fucked by you! I think I'm being more than fair, I'm willing to pay you for your services."

"Then I'm going to tell all of our little secrets."

"It'll be your word against mine, and who would believe you over me? All I have to do is make everyone believe you are demon-possessed, and then shit will really be fucked up for you. I'll see you at Bible Study tonight." He says as he turns to walk away.

Can you believe the nerve of him? He's just made the biggest mistake of his life, underestimating me. Now I really need to get a massage. On my way to *Heavenly Touch* I hear someone call my name, and I turn to see Dorian walking over to me.

"Hey beautiful."

"Hey."

"Where are you on your way to?"

"To *Heavenly Touch*."

"I can give you a heavenly touch for free, and I'm sure you will enjoy it more."

"Ok…"

"What?" Dorian is completely caught off guard.

"Let's do it. Dorian, these last few days have been bizarre for me, and I'm tired of pretending to be someone I'm not. You were right, the only way I can be truly happy is if I'm real."

I take Dorian's hand in mine before I continue. "The real me has been wanting to do a lot of nasty, freaky things with you for a long time now. After Sunday night, I've thought about you a lot. I'm tired of playing games, let's go to the *Hillside*."

"What about Aaron?"

"Fuck Aaron! He's not the man I thought he was; I'm not the woman he thinks I am. I'm tired of all his bullshit, tired of him trying to control me. I'm a grown ass woman and I can do as I please, and right now I want to fuck you Dorian."

"I'm glad you're finally freeing yourself. Aaron will be hurt though, and quite frankly, I don't want to fuck you."

"What?! You let me stand here and pour out my heart to you and now you don't want to fuck me? FUCK YOU DORIAN!!!!"

I storm off towards *Heavenly Touch*. Dorian runs up behind me and grabs my arm.

"Arian, you didn't let me finish. I don't want to fuck you."

"You said that already!"

"I want to make love to you girl."

The way that he spoke and the look of passion in his eyes almost had me in tears, no man has ever looked at me like that before. Not even Aaron. His eyes told me that it was more than lust

-Chapter 9-

Judgment Day is the only way to describe my last service. It was anything but blessed and anointed. I'm so happy! I can never show my face in that church again. A couple of days before, Elise went to Deacon Anderson to follow through with our plan. She tried reasoning with him, but he wasn't hearing it. He even threatened her again. What he didn't know is that she had a tape recorder on her and recorded everything.

Pastor Young had no clue that our little chit chat at the mall the other day was recorded. Elise and the sound technician at the church used to fuck, so she convinced him to play our tapes during service when she gave him the signal.

The Praise and Worship leader wants me, so it wasn't hard to convince him to do things a little differently also. When the good Deacon heard his voice on that tape he tried his best to get at Elise. He really looked like he was going to try to kill her. It took four other deacons to hold him down.

Then came Pastor Young's tape, he simply fainted. Once he came to, he was knocked back out by my brother Alex, the Minister of Music. Alex was pissed because he thought that he was the only man that Pastor Young was boning. Come to find out, he was boning all the men on the Praise Team! What a hot ass mess, they all took turns beating his ass.

About twenty minutes later, the police showed up and made some arrests. Pastor Young was arrested also for statutory rape.

Turns out it wasn't too late to press charges, and they had all the proof they needed other than his nut all in me.

You may be wondering why Elise and I put ourselves out there like that. We are tired of people praising these men like they're as good as God. When in reality, they ain't shit. It was time for them to get what they had coming to them. Yes, we put ourselves out there in the process, but to us it was all worth it.

As for Aaron, I haven't seen or heard from him in a while. Pastor Evan's son must have given him a heads-up. After he heard about what we did to Pastor Young and Deacon Anderson, I think he is trying to stay as far away from me as possible, which is fine with me.

Dorian and I are becoming very close, and he is blowing my back out every chance he gets. It feels so good being around someone that I can totally be me with. We're always up for experiencing new things. He even got me to go to a titty bar with him. That's not really my scene, but it was something different. Maybe I can get him to go to a male strip club with me, but I doubt it. I'm getting the best of both worlds, the buddy and the booty. He truly makes me happy.

The Pleasure of Sin

Written by Arie Olah

-Chapter 1-

"Amen! Amen!" said Pastor Spinks. "The doors of the Church are now open. We are extending an Invitation for Salvation, and as the choir sings softly, I want you to search your hearts and consider what God has for you."

The choir begins to sing at a low volume of how excellent the Lord's name is.

"Come on, Salvation is yours right now," continues Pastor Spinks. "You never know what tomorrow may bring. Give your life to God today so you can see His face in peace."

Amens are yelled from all sides as the church begins to applaud. A young woman in a red dress that was sexy, but not too revealing stood up. Many of the self-righteous older women of the church scowled at her. But Talisha kept her head held high as she walked down the center aisle along with the others that chose the Lord.

Deacon Redd turns to Deacon Stone and whispers, "Damn she's fine! I would love to hit that."

"Not before him," Deacon Stone says gesturing to the pulpit where Pastor Spinks stood. The two old men share a chuckle.

"What is she wearing?" Sister Smith asks Sister Louis.

"It's a shame is what it is, just a shame," is Janie Louis' response.

Pastor Spinks was taken aback by Talisha's beauty as she got closer to him. He'd seen her visit the church on several occasions but didn't approach because of the gossip queens that attend the church. He was so engrossed in thought, that he almost forgot where he was. Thankfully, he was wearing a robe today; otherwise everyone would know exactly what he was thinking.

"Good afternoon Pastor Spinks and Church Family," says Sister Moses the church secretary as she announced those who were joining *Christ Chapel* today. The names of the Baptismal Candidates were announced after them.

"Hello Sister Reyes, we are honoured to name you as a member of *Christ Chapel.* And just as I've welcomed all of the others, I must ask you the same questions. First, do you believe that Jesus Christ died for your sins?"

"Yes, I do," Talisha spoke with tears in her eyes.

"Now this question is the most important one."

A few *Amens* rang out from the congregation.

"Do you accept the Lord Jesus Christ as your own Personal Saviour?"

"Yes," she replied through even more tears.

"Thank You Jesus! We've been truly blessed here with six new members, three of which wish to be baptized."

Many in the congregation began shouting and praising the Lord as the pastor spoke.

"The Lord told me not to wait, so I am asking you three if you would like to baptized right here and now?"

Two candidates said *yes*, while the third wanted to wait for his family to be in attendance.

-Chapter 2-

"I can't believe you baptized that woman like that today! You know she wasn't prepared!" Sister Spinks yelled exasperatedly at her husband.

"What are you talking about?" he asked in a non-interested tone.

"I'm talking about you disrespecting me time and time again. You could see right through her robe when she came up out of the water!"

"Are you saying I was wrong for bringing one more lost soul closer to God?"

"You know what the hell I mean! Don't try and flip this!"

"Hey, I gave her an option," he said shrugging his shoulders. Anyway, I didn't see you complain about the young man before her."

"Whatever! Just know I will not be disrespected. And why do you have to do the baptizing, I thought the Assistant Pastor was hired for that type of stuff?"

"Look, I'm the Pastor and I do as I want, when I want," he says dismissively.

"I won't stand for this anymore," is her stern warning.

"What are you going to do, leave me?" he asks while laughing.

"I just might Jon!"

"I don't care what you do, or even when you do it."

"Jon!"

"Later for this, I have someplace to be right now."

"Where are you going? We just got home! And we're not finished talking."

"Goodbye."

"Answer me, where are you going? You can't just leave like this!"

Bothered by the incessant yelling, Pastor Spinks grabbed his wife by her arms. She screams for him to let her go. Sister Spinks had never seen her husband like that before. Jon usually only yelled, he'd never gotten physical with her before. She found herself being forced to bend over the arm of the living room couch. Jon then forced her dress up, and tore away her panties like an animal. Glenda was turned on yet frightened, as she begged him to stop. This was met by her head being shoved down into the couch's pillows. Pastor Spinks dropped his pants and shoved his dick in her so hard she no longer protested. Sister Spinks moaned with pleasure as she was being pounded.

He fucked her as if she was an object, a shell without feeling. Jon was trying to fuck her so hard so that, he wouldn't have to hear her voice again. Pastor Spinks shot his load on her back, in her hair, and on the couch. He then smacked Glenda on the ass and told her to clean it all up. Sister Spinks was dazed but happy as she lay on the couch and went to sleep.

-Chapter 3-

An hour later, Jon pulled up next her car. Talisha had been instructed to meet him at a park thirty minutes away from the church. He unlocked the car doors and she got in the back seat. The black *Lexus* with its soft and creamy leather seats turned her on instantly. She felt herself getting moist.

"So do you always meet your women this way?"

"Sshh!" Pastor Spinks said placing his fingers to his lips.

"Please do not ruin this for yourself."

For some reason, this made him even sexier. His voice put her in a deep trance. The man's lips were something out of a movie, while his eyes were soft and comforting like brown marbles. With skin the color of mocha, had he not been a pastor, he could have easily been a model. Or a damn good pimp. The kind she wouldn't mind giving all her money to.

As they road in silence, Pastor Spinks thought of the things he wanted to do to the girl. First, he wished he could remember her name.

Why are women so easy? He wonders while glancing at her in the rear view mirror. *They just do whatever I tell them to. She wore no makeup as I requested, no perfume, just a slight hint of Vanilla Brown Sugar Body Wash. This is too easy.*

She smiled when she saw him looking at her in the rear-view mirror. Licking her lips, she unbuttoned the rest of the buttons on her blouse, revealing a lace black and red bra, she'd been asked her to wear. For morning service, Talisha had on a hot pink bra and panty set that was seen by all when she was baptized. She began to gently stroke her cleavage. His dick, rock hard, was begging to be let out.

Diverting his eyes from her, Jon checked his mirrors again to make sure he wasn't being followed. He was very careful not to let anyone know about the car he purchased a year ago. It was kept at a private self parking storage lot.

Arriving at *Christ Chapel*, Pastor Spinks drove around the block to make sure none of his sheep were there doing whatever it was they did. When he was satisfied that the coast was clear, he parked in the rear of the church.

Leading her into the church's auditorium, he tells Talisha how beautiful she looks.

"Thank you Pastor," she gushes.

"I've been watching you for awhile," he states.

"And I have been checking you out as well."

"So that explains why you wear those low-cut tops and short skirts almost every time you visit."

"Well, I had to do something to get your attention," she answers frankly. "But I didn't think you ever noticed."

"Yeah, I noticed," Jon says flashing a bright smile.

"Pastor, now that I have you all alone there's something I've wanted to do for some time now."

"Really? What, may I ask?"

"Kiss you."

"What are you waiting for, "he asks opening his arms in invitation.

"Ok, but I want to kiss you in the pulpit at your podium," Talisha says coyly.

"Sure, but I have one rule before you enter my pulpit."

"And that is?"

"You must remove your clothing."

Kissing him was just as she had imagined it would be. It was like tasting caramel. She was getting wet with anticipation. Talisha felt her nipples harden as Jon pulled her closer to him. Pastor Spinks' erection was evident in their tight embrace.

Being inquisitive, she had to see it for herself, so she began to slowly pull away from him. In one smooth motion, the young lady dropped to her knees, and quickly undid his trousers.

"Whatever you have in there looks like it needs to be rescued."

Pastor Spinks looks down at her because he loved the look of shock and awe on his conquests' faces when they view his penis for the first time. And just as expected, this one was no exception.

"Wow!" she exclaims while taking his thick, beautiful brown dick in hand. Not wasting any time, she took him inside her mouth. Relaxing her throat, Sister Reyes took as much she could. She wanted him to know that she wasn't scared of all that he had to offer.

They always moan she thought, but Pastor Spinks didn't make a sound. So she went to working her mouth like a pro. Grabbing

Talisha's hair, Jon fed his dick to her hard. He was impressed that she could keep up.

Damn, they all want to be the best, he thinks with a slight chuckle. Still sucking vigorously, Talisha is pulled by her hair as her Reverend moves to his chair in the pulpit. She didn't seem to notice or mind that this was happening.

Damn! This bitch can suck while crawling! She's really putting in work. Thrusting his pelvis up, Jon releases his load down her throat. Talisha didn't let a drop of his semen escape her lips. *Oh! This bitch wants a repeat session. Such a shame*, he thinks.

"Pastor Spinks, can I please sit on your dick?" she asks still on her knees in front of him and licking her lips.

Without answering, he reaches into a side of compartment in his chair and pulls out a condom.

"Wait," she says holding up her hand. "Do you do this a lot?"

-CHAPTER 4-

Resisting the urge to slap Sister Reyes, Pastor Jon Spinks says simply, "I see you're talking again. Maybe my dick needs to be in your mouth some more? Your choice, ride this dick or talk…" Standing to her feet, Talisha begins to straddle him.

"I just think its weird you being a pastor and all, having condoms in the pulpit."

"Baby, I just like to be prepared that's all. Now as you can see, my dick is hard again. You riding or leaving?"

With a devilish smile, she turns her back to him and bends over slowly while removing her panties. This is to make sure the Pastor gets a good look at her ass and wet pussy. Dancing slowly and seductively, Talisha deftly unsnaps her brassiere.

Implants! This bitch has implants! Jon is surprised to discover.

Unsure as to how she was going to handle such a big dick, Talisha mounted him tentatively. Once he was inside of her, she was sure she had never been opened like Pastor Spinks had her. As her pussy began to accommodate his girth, she rode like it was the last dick she would ever feel. Oddly, he never broke a sweat.

After the second orgasm, Sister Reyes lost count of how many times she came.

"Damn Pastor! I never knew fucking you would be this good!"

You're talking again! Is his thought as he neared ejaculation. Suddenly and without warning, Jon stands up, dumping Talisha to the floor.

"Get in the chair on your knees and grab the back of it," he gruffly commands.

Like it is her duty, she quickly scrambles to his chair. With her plump juicy ass offered up to him like a tithe, Pastor Spinks shoves his dick inside her vagina from behind. Gripping her waist, his balls smack against her ass cheeks as he grinds and pumps away.

Damn, I just fucked my wife like this. I ain't shit!

"Yes Pastor! Fuck me harder!"

Talisha's screams of ecstasy, break him away from his thoughts.

"Now this talking I like!" He says banging her still harder. He began pulling her hair as she begged for more. When Jon felt himself ready to explode, he pulled out of her sopping wet pussy, pulled off the condom and nutted all over her back.

The royally fucked woman struggled to her feet, and reached for her still moist panties.

"Where do you think you're going? I'm not through with that ass," Pastor Spinks stated.

"Yeah, right", the young woman retorts.

Annoyed, the Right Reverend grabs Talisha's wrist, and quickly leads her to the baptismal pool.

Damn! This man is sexy as fuck! She thinks as he removes his shirt. Being manhandled like this was turning Sister Reyes on even more. After leading her into the pool, Jon pulls her close.

"This morning I wanted to shove my fingers inside you like this," he says, finger fucking her.

She moans as his fingers slide in. Talisha was enjoying the way he touched her.

"Then I wanted to press you up against this glass and fuck you," he whispers into her ear.

"Fuck me again Pastor Spinks," she says in a lust filled voice. Before she knows it, his penis is wrapped in a fresh condom and sliding inside her. The feeling of being fucked underwater was electrifying.

Where did he get that condom from? She wondered but didn't ask.

Again, no passion, just fucking. How many times have I cum today? And what time is it anyway? Jon wondered.

Talisha was moaning and screaming his name like he'd forgotten it. He was hoping to one day find his sexual equal, someone to match his performance, someone that would make him cum and fall asleep.

As Pastor Spinks fucked Sister Reyes in the baptismal pool, he looked out into his empty church thinking of all the women he had screwed in this very position, and the ones he planned on nailing. Many of them thought he'd leave his wife for them.

Dumb bitches! Even those down low niggas want this dick, but I'll never give up on pussy.

He recalled when he first saw this one. *Damn, what is her name?* The *Forgotten One* was still moaning and splashing as the Man of God penetrated her time and time again. Pastor Spinks changed position to one of his favorites. Pressing her against the back wall of the pool, he picked her up and she wrapped her legs around him as she received his erection. *It's good being me!* He says to himself while looking at the mirror above. Jon admired himself as he fucked away.

"Goddamn Pastor! You're killin' this pussy! Fuck... me... harder! Please don't stop!" Talisha pleaded. "Ooohhh! Pastor Spinks this is your pussy! Take it...get it!"

Damn, another one, he thinks as he slows his pace.

"Get on your knees at the steps."

When her round ass is in the right position, he resumes stroking in and out of her pussy. Several moments later, Jon pulls out and snatches the condom off. Taking his penis in hand, he shoots what little he has left onto Talisha's back.

"I now indeed baptise you as a new member of the *Pastor Spinks' Dick Committee,*" he says his now famous line.

-CHAPTER 5-

After allowing Sister Reyes a few minutes to dress, Pastor Spinks drives her back to her car. He then explains the rules on how to keep getting some of his dick. If Talisha doesn't comply she will be cut off.

"Whatever you say Pastor, I'll agree to it."

Before Jon lets her out, he checks her purse to make sure she wasn't recording anything.

Pastor Jon Spinks returned to *Christ Chapel* to drain the pool. After showering in his office, he retrieved the videotape of his session with Talisha. He watched it as he called a few of the Sick and Shut-in members to check on and pray for them. Amazingly, watching the video made him hard again. After the phone calls, Jon decides that next week's sermon will be on forgiveness. So he writes out a few notes and calls it a night.

Before returning home, Pastor Jon stops at *Meijer* for a dozen roses. As soon as he walks in, he presents the flowers to Glenda, and apologizes for his earlier actions. Much to Sister Spinks' dismay, her husband promises it will never happen again, mainly because he knew she liked it.

Ha! You will never receive that much pleasure from me again. He says to himself about his wife.

"Jon, where did all of that aggression come from this afternoon?" she asks him as they lie in bed.

"Who knows? Maybe it was the Devil," he answers while gently kissing her. Pastor Spinks then makes love softly in the

Missionary position to Glenda before rolling over and falling asleep.

Lost In Eden

By: Anthony Striggles

-Chapter 1-

How has it come to this? You ask yourself as your penis disappears impossibly into her mouth. You think you'd never be one of *those* types of men. And at first, you actually were of strong moral fiber. But, no *butt,* how often is a man expected to withstand temptation? As a child you were brought up to believe that the *Holy Ghost* would magically keep your lusts in check. You eventually learned that only the wetness of a woman could extinguish your raging loin fire; and what a *Body of Water* kneeling before you today.

Your groans, grunts and moans signal to Jeanette that your release is soon to come. She ceases her deep-throating, and begins sucking vigorously on the head of your penis. The extreme sensation of this coupled with the firm gripping of her hand on your shaft, makes you erupt into Jeanette's mouth like a volcano. And as on previous occasions, this beautiful young woman swallows your seed. Jeanette kisses your penis head as it spasms with the last of your ejaculation. She then takes a damp towel and cleanses your testicles and penis of her saliva.

"Damn, that was good babe."

Jeanette just gives you a naughty smile as she stands and straightens her clothes.

"Well I'm gonna catch a few winks before the Board Meeting, just tell everyone I'm outta the office, ok?"

"Not a problem," she says as she turns to leave your office. "Pastor, what do I tell the First Lady when she calls?"

"Just tell her I'm in a counseling session."

As the door closes, you recline once more in your burgundy executive chair by *Bagina*, and you ponder how a girl so young could be such a champion at giving head. Jeanette's 22 years should not produce that level of proficiency. You determine that she may be another victim of sexual abuse. You then shudder as you wonder if she regards you as her father, or some older man who may have taken advantage of her.

"Wow, I hope not," you say aloud as you drift off to sleep.

-Chapter 2-

As you enter the conference room, the sycophants that are scattered about disgust you. You manufacture a smile for each and every Board member as you greet them, and take your seat at the head of the lavish mahogany table.

"I want to thank you all for coming out on such short notice. I have two major issues that I'd like to discuss this evening."

You pause for effect and slowly sweep your head around the room to make visual contact with all twelve eyes that are present.

"Firstly, we have met our quota for the expansion and renovation project." You begin to applaud this feat, and all of your puppets do likewise.

"Now, this information is to remain in this room because we will still be receiving pledge money until January."

You see the looks of confusion upon their faces, so you reach for the pitcher of water at the center of the table. You deliberately take your time as you pick up the overturned crystal goblet from the linen napkin it rests upon. As you pour the cold iced water, you never look at any of the Board members. After taking a sip from the goblet, you then look around the room again. As usual, there are no challengers.

"Now, this brings me to the second order of business. Some of you may know that the *Motown In the Spirit Music Festival*, that's held every summer in *Hart Plaza,* has been canceled due to a lack of corporate funding. I want *Eden Worship Center* to completely fund the festival this year."

"How Pastor Browne?"

You see that Deacon Harper has finally found his testes.

"I'm glad you asked. The Building Project funds will be allocated for the festival. In addition, once it has been made public that the proverbial show will go on, I'm relatively sure that some of the other churches in the city will want to contribute also, which will lessen the load."

You sit back in your chair to let your plan marinate in the minds of the Board.

Unbeknownst to them, you've personally taken out a $250,000 loan for the expansion and renovation. Because you were able to pay off the church's 30-year mortgage in 6 years, the bank saw no problem with extending you a quarter-million dollar line of credit. You've sold the church on not getting a loan, but raising the funds "by faith." Now, your debt will be totally repaid in only 8 months. This essentially will ensure you a new line of at least one million dollars.

"I think it's a great idea Pastor! Not only will it be good for the community, it'll be excellent publicity for *Eden,*" Sister Taylor says excitedly.

"You know, I hadn't even considered the publicity the festival would bring," you say, which of course is a bold-faced lie.

"It's not about me. I just want to bring glory to the Kingdom of God Sister Taylor."

Your years of experience in *Church-Speak*, allow for you to effortlessly serve up clichés that for some reason inspire the listener.

-Chapter 3-

You wonder how you even manage to maintain an erection for
these sessions. Your wife, although beautiful, turns you on as

much as the act of snatching out your pubic hair while it's dry. You only wedded her to further your aspirations as a clergyman. She's great *arm-furniture*. Thanks be to God, Donyetta couldn't bear any children. You look down at your wife in pity as you ram her repeatedly, and wonder how she can pretend that you actually love her. The contempt for Donyetta causes you to quicken your pelvic thrusts and release what little semen Jeanette left into your wife. You roll over to catch your breath, and while staring at the ceiling, your cell phone rings.

Reaching onto the nightstand alongside the bed you pick it up seeing Deacon Harper's name displayed.

"Hello?"

"Pastor Browne, you and I need to have a sit-down."

Equally surprised and intrigued by the Deacon's tone you bite.

"Ok, what's on your mind?"

"I'll tell you tomorrow at your office. Is noon good?"

"Noon will be fine, see you tomorrow Deacon Harper."

After you place your cell back on the nightstand you play certain scenarios in your mind that you may be faced with tomorrow. After about fifteen minutes realize you need to get some rest in order to have your wits about you. Opening your nightstand drawer a vodka filled flask is grabbed. After two quick hits, you feel the warming of your blood by the alcohol. Soon after, a deep sleep envelopes you.

-Chapter 4-

"Jeanette, take the rest of the day off. Go get a manicure, pedicure and massage on me," you say handing her 3 crisp hundred-dollar bills.

"Thank you Pastor. Just call me if you need anything."

"You know I will baby, now scoot!"

Not wanting any witnesses of the meeting with Deacon Harper, you send Jeanette away watching her leave the building from your closed-circuit security camera monitor. You then check to make sure everything is setup before the deacon's arrival.

Whatever is on Deacon Harper's mind is serious, because he is ten minutes earlier than scheduled. Smilingly shrewdly, you stand to open the office door.

"Dennis, come on in and close the door so we won't be disturbed. Would you like a beverage?"

"Pastor Browne let's cut the pleasantries. I'm here for one reason and one reason only."

"And what is that Deacon Harper?"

"It's simple, I want in."

"*In?*" you ask feigning ignorance.

"Yes, I want a cut of the skim."

"Skim? I don't know…"

Deacon Harper raises a hand curtly to silence your attempted denial.

"Just stop, I've been watching and waiting for an opportunity, and last night's meeting showed me."

"Dennis have a seat," you say to regain a modicum of authority.

"Now just what are you talking about?"

"The Building Fund will be a good place to start," he says cockily.

"Deacon Harper, the funds collected are ear-marked for the *Motown In The Spirit Music Festival.*"

Deacon Dennis Harper moves to the edge of his seat before speaking.

"Look, you and I both know that you're just going to personally assume the financing for the festival, which will be written off as a charitable donation on your taxes. Not only that, you've more than likely already cut a side deal with the city so that their take is at least 10-percent less than what the budget actually calls for. How's that for starters?"

Sitting back in your recliner, you regard this man with new found respect. Deacon Harper has hit the nail squarely on the head. Although in actuality, you were able to convince the city to take 30- percent off. Not only that, you've also brokered a 5-percent cut from *Supreme Sound and Stage.* They stood to lose too much money on the canceled 3-day event, so they were more than willing to pay your price.

"Well Dennis, what you are suggesting could be viewed as embezzlement, wouldn't you say?"

"I couldn't give a damn! You've been getting fat off of this cash cow for far too long. It's time to share the wealth. If not, I'm sure the members of *Eden* won't be too happy to know that they're funds are being misappropriated."

"Ok, ok, yes the city did agree to give me a break, but it's only 5- percent. I'm willing to give half of that to you Deacon Harper for your cooperation."

"You're giving me too much, too easily Browne, you have another angle."

"Deacon Harper, true I am offering you half, but the whole deal is contingent upon the funds from the Building Project. So in essence, you have me by the short-n-curlies," you say with a wry smile.

"I don't believe or trust you Browne, but I will take half."

"Well it's settled then." Standing you extend your right hand to cement the agreement.

"I'll be expecting my cut within the week Pastor Browne," you are told as Deacon Harper shakes your hand.

"Dennis, you're playing hard ball, that's for sure."

"No, I just need for you to know how serious I am Browne."

You raise both of your hands in a sign of surrender.

"Ok, ok, I believe you. Just give me two days."

"Two days it is then. I'll be in touch Pastor Browne."

Watching as Deacon Dennis Harper smugly turns and walks out of your office, you return to your desk and the security monitor to watch him exit the building. When the deacon's automobile is no longer visible on the screen, the next move is to close and lock the office door.

The custom Maplewood bookshelf next to the now closed door has what appears to be an ornamental seashell paperweight. You then disconnect two hidden wires from the back of the seashell. Upon returning to your desk, you remove a pair of ear bud headphones from a drawer. Deacon Harper's blackmail demands sound crystal clear on the Voice-Activated Digital Micro-Recorder you purchased from the *Spy Shop*. It was money well spent.

-Chapter 5-

"How can you expect to prosper without investment? A farmer doesn't expect a harvest at the end of the season if he hasn't planted anything. Not a sane one at any rate. I can't walk into *Fifth*

Third Bank and withdraw money from them if I haven't an account there with deposited funds can I? Well, I could, but that's a federal crime in this country."

You have fully captivated your audience. This, the last of two services today, is filled to capacity. You know that the usual haul for tithes and offerings is around 140,000 dollars per week, but after you're finished, 200 grand will be reachable.

"Why do you expect anything from the King if you don't invest in His Kingdom?"

You allow the emotional waves of excitement to subside before continuing.

"I want you to turn to the person seated next to you, and ask, *What have you given to the Kingdom?*"

Numerous people make their way to the front of the auditorium, and begin to throw money on the steps that lead up to the podium.

"Have you sold out for Christ?"

You see hundreds of hands raise signifying their allegiance to God.

"You can't sell out for something you haven't invested in."
Thunderous applause and uproarious *amen-ing* punctuate your point, but you see resistance in many faces as you scan the vast audience, so you know you must continue.

"I know that some of you may be thinking that I'm just preaching this to get your money, but Pastor Browne doesn't need your money! I'm just trying to get you blessed! Those negative thoughts you're receiving are straight from the Pits of Hell! It's

Satan's desire and design to see you remain broke, busted and disgusted! But Jesus came so you will have life! And not just life, but life in abundance! And as our perfect example, Christ said that it's better to give than to receive. And He showed it on Calvary's Old Rugged Cross."

You have them precisely where you want them. *Eden Worship Center* is in frenzied state as you prance from one side of the platform to the other.

"Without faith, it's impossible to please God. And faith is a verb, because faith without works is nothing! Faith without works is dead! Today is your opportunity to give life to your faith."

You pause as you survey your handiwork. Five, ten, twenty and fifty dollar bills along with personal checks lay strewn about your Ostrich Oxfords. Then, to further solidify the importance of this moment, you close your eyes and nod your head several times.

"Yes, yes," you say as if you are agreeing with someone.

"Listen, the Lord just revealed to me that the reason some of you have not experienced true prosperity in your lives, is because you won't exercise your faith! He's saying right now to *Eden Worship Center*, that you have to work the faith for the faith to work!

The thousands in attendance erupt in uproarious fashion to your freshly revealed words straight from *Heaven's Throne Room*. With the smoothness of a veteran preacher, you signal the lead musician to begin softly playing the verse to a song penned by you.

"Like a seed never plan-ted.

It's power of life never gran-ted.

So is the gift of faith within yo-u-u!

The electricity of expectation is rolling through the auditorium as the "Faith-for-Funds" anthem is sung by your faithful.

"Sister LaVette, come on up and minister to us. And as she comes in her own way, any of you who haven't sown a faith seed yet, this is the time to do so; especially while the Prosperity *Anointing* is so heavy in this place."

-Chapter 6-

"Harper, while I admire your gumption for attempting to extort from me, I'll have to tell you to go fuck yourself," you say with a wicked sneer.

"Pastor Browne, let's cut the pleasantries, I'm here for one reason and one reason only."

"And what is that Deacon Harper?"

"It's simple, I want to skim The Building Fund."

"Skim? I don't know…"

"Just stop, I've been watching and waiting for an opportunity, and last night's meeting showed me."

"Well Dennis, what you are suggesting could be viewed as embezzlement, wouldn't you say?"

"I couldn't give a damn! I'll be expecting my cut within the week Pastor Browne."

You let the air settle between you and Deacon Harper as you press the stop button on the digital recorder.

"You slimy bastard! You know that didn't go down like that!" Deacon Harper rages.

"Ha! But who can prove otherwise? Who's going to believe you over *The Mand of Gawd?*" you ask laughing derisively in Deacon Harper's grimacing face.

"There's a special place in Hell for your ass Browne," he says through clenched teeth.

"Now, now Harper, there's really no need for all of that. Plus, the Word says that He isn't willing that anyone should perish, and we all know that nothing supersedes God's Will."

Deacon Harper abruptly stands up to leave your office.

"Hey, wait! I have a consolation prize for you Dennis."

Deacon Harper pauses at the door without opening it.

"Console these nuts!" He seethes as he grabs his crotch, pulling it three times to emphasize each word.

"Whoa! I think you need to remember I have your nuts right here in my hand," you remind him by brandishing the doctored recording. "Now sit your bitter ass down and listen to me."

Quickly realizing the validity of your not so subtle threat, Deacon Dennis Harper slowly returns to his seat like a man defeated.

"Dennis, I agree to your initial demand, but with one caveat. Without awaiting his response, you shove a stack of forms across your desk to him.

"You are to become the Chairman of the Board for my Foundation. You will get a new home and automobile that the Foundation will own, as well as other perks."

"Why are you being so generous Browne?" he asks, questioning your motives.

"It's simple, I need a tax shelter from the IRS, and I need somewhere to put my money so my wife can't get it whenever I decide to divorce her pitiful ass. And since you've shown me you can be a *go-getta* as the young folk say, you'll do perfectly. Not to mention, I'm sure you don't want this recording to fall into the hands of the authorities."

"You are a piece of work Browne. Where do I sign?"

-Chapter 7-

"Lee! Will you at least give me the courtesy of pretending you have a wife?" Donyetta asks irritably.

Your shoulders shrug as if to say, *whatever*.

"Donyetta, I'm married not blind. You saw how her good-ities and nice-ities were all splayed for the world to see."

"You're a pastor Lee you can't act like everyone else."

"Look, just shut up and go buy your damn outfit for the conference. I've told you about all that lip. You don't tell your Head what to do," you say just loud enough not to cause a scene in the Somerset Mall. "And remember my color scheme. I don't want you messin' up my vibe."

In two days, you and the First Lady will be flying to Baltimore where you will be ministering at *The Mountain Moving Faith Conference*. The Crème De La Crème of Churchdom will be in attendance. You grin as you envision the theatrical performance you have planned.

This is the event that will make your career as a Pulpiteer. You recall how a female Evangelist rose from virtual obscurity when she did the now famous "Make Up Your Bed" sermon at the conference. She's since parlayed that into millions of dollars.

"Pastor Browne! Praise the Lord!"

Shaking you from your reverie is quite possibly the loudest speaking woman this side of Heaven.

"Sister Cantrell! How are you?"

"Blessed and highly favored Pastor!" she bellows as if you two are half a football field apart.

You try not to cringe as she assails you with her loudness.

"It's so good to see you! Me and my daughter Irene are just out here shopping a taste."

You chuckle slightly because whenever Sister Cantrell mentions her daughter, it's always "My Daughter Irene."

"It's good to be seen," is all you muster in response.

Fortunately, your wife suddenly exits the store she went into.

"Over here baby!," is your cry for help.

Donyetta looks at you quizzically before she notices Sister Cantrell. She then quickly realizes what's up.

"Hey Sister Cantrell! Will you please keep my husband company while I run into *Macy's* to grab a purse?" Donyetta asks not waiting for a response. "Thank you, I won't be long."

Your wife gives you a great big smile and a wink.

"See ya honey."

"Well Pastor, since weez here, I got some thangs I been meaning ta ask ya."

Where is the Rapture when you need it? You wonder to yourself.

"Why don't you bless the new wee babies on the altar like Bishop Hemlock usta?"

"Sister Cantrell, The Bible never has commanded that we christen our children. That practice is derived from Child Sacrifice, where people once sacrificed their children to various Gods. So, I don't feel it necessary to continue such a barbaric ritual."

You watch as her eyes begin to glass over. You can almost hear what you've just said as it bounces off of her traditional mindset.

"But Bishop Hemlock said…"

You raise your right hand to stop her in mid-sentence.

"Bishop Hemlock and his teachings were for his time. Life is a constant progression Sister Cantrell."

"And why you be lettin' womens come inta God's House wif pants on? Dat's a shame fo' God! Bishop Hemlock neva woulda let no mess gwan like at!"

"Sister Cantrell, you and the good Bishop Hemlock must've missed the passage where JESUS said that we aren't to let people judge us by what we eat, drink, or wear, because none of those things matter as far as God's Kingdom is concerned. And since I call myself a CHRISTian and not a HEMLOCKian, I'll be following what Jesus said," you say with finality. "Well there's my wife. You have a good afternoon Sister Cantrell."

-Chapter 8-

"Damn J! When you gon' quit frontin' and give a nigga da ass?!"

"When you learn to speak to a lady properly."

"You always on dat *proper* bullshit. Yo ass ackin' all uppity and shit."

"DaRell, just because you choose to *Keep it Real Illiterate*, it doesn't mean I have to."

"Fuck u bitch! I'm gettin' dis paper. Dat's all dat matters. If you wuz bout yours, you wouldn't still be pushin' dat raggedy ass Corsica round dis bitch," D-Rell says as he peels off in his convertible white Dodge Charger with 24-inch chrome wheels.

Jeanette has to laugh aloud at D-Rell's assessment of her. If only he knew that she'd been masterminding a major come up for herself for the last several months. As the secretary for *Eden Worship Center*, Jeanette had been privy to quite a few of Pastor Browne's schemes. So when she'd been directed to order a Voice Activated Digital Micro Recorder, she ordered two. The day after Deacon Harper was blackmailed into signing on as Chairman for Pastor Browne's Non-Profit organization; Jeanette could hardly contain herself as she listened to the recordings. Now a waiting game had to be played before she could use the information to her advantage.

Jeanette grew up in Cincinnati as the only child of a prominent minister and his wife. Her father became pastor of *Lighthouse Cathedral of Faith* when she was but a toddler. As she grew she'd heard rumors of his philandering. But ironically nothing was ever brought to light at *Lighthouse Cathedral of Faith*. By the time Jeanette reached adolescence, Bishop Taylor and his wife were sleeping in separate beds.

Jeanette excelled in academics while in high school. School was her escape from the reality of her home life. The young Ms. Taylor received a full academic scholarship to the University of Michigan.

It was in her sophomore year right before Spring Break, that Jeanette received a call at the Stockwell dorms that her father had suddenly passed. The widow Taylor had already booked a flight on Northwest for Jeanette. All she had to do was take the fifteen minute shuttle bus ride from Ann Arbor to Metro Airport.

Jeanette had to sit next to her mother and listen as countless people extolled the virtues of the late great Bishop Jesse P. Taylor at his Homegoing services. All the while, both women wondered how they were going to survive. Jeanette's father left the church and entire estate to his lover/secretary. Jeanette knew her mother hadn't been saving for a rainy day, so contesting the will would prove quite difficult. That fateful day, Jeanette vowed to herself that she would never be caught without a plan in the future.

-Chapter 9-

"Please stand with me and welcome the speaker for this evening, a preacher in his own right. Coming to us by way of Detroit, Michigan, Pastor Lee Browne!" The rousing introduction was given by none other than the great, Bishop I.P. Lakes, who served as conference host. The auditorium reverberates with the sound of thousands of pairs of hands clapping. The heat from the television lights has caused a thin sheet of perspiration to form along your brow. You dab it away with an *LB* monogrammed white handkerchief as you stand.

The chestnut brown, custom made four- button single-breasted *Rosco Melvin* suit remains unwrinkled, much to your delight. The exclusive designer is definitely worth his price tags. The crisp French blue shirt with its French cuffs, perfectly compliment your dark orange and navy blue horizontally striped tie. Cognac colored alligator loafers complete the ensemble. You know that you've chosen well by the apprising looks of the other clergymen. Purposefully, you stride to the rostrum. Your *armor bearer*, or personal valet as he should more accurately be called, rushes from his seat with your bible, a small navy blue towel with *LB* embroidered in gold, and a glass of cool water.

"Come on, let's worship Him!" you urge the attendees.

The volume in the convention center rises.

"That would be alright if it was for me, but I'm talking about JEEE-sus!" Your goading illicits an uproarious response from clergy and laity alike.

"There's none like Him! From the rising of the sun, until the going down of the same, He's worthy of our praise."

As the *Thank you Lords* and *Hallelujahs* are sent to Heaven, you situate the bible and glass of water.

"You may be seated in the presence of Almighty God."

A hush settles in as the multitude is seated.

"To Bishop and Elect Lady Lakes, all of the distinguished men and women of God seated behind me on the pulpit, and to all of the saints, I greet you in the matchless name of our Lord and Savior, Jesus Christ. I count it an honor and privilege to stand before you on such an auspicious occasion."

As any suck-up worth their weight, you turn to Bishop I.P. Lakes and nod your head as a sign of gratitude and respect.

"I would be remiss if I didn't mention the apple of my eye, my lovely wife of ten years. Please stand babe," you request as you place both hands to your mouth to blow a kiss. There is the obligatory applause as Donyetta rises from her seat. Her eyes sparkle as she returns the blown kiss.

Like a good orator, you pause for effect.

"How many of you under the sound of my voice need a Right-Now Word," you ask while raising your right hand in the air. There is a resounding chorus of *yes* as well as countless upraised hands as answers to your question.

"Let's reverence the reading of God's Word by standing please. Turn with me to the third chapter of the Book of Genesis. We'll start reading at verse seven."

You wait several moments to allow the people to locate the text, and then in your best *James Earl Jones* voice you read.

"Then the eyes of both of them were opened, and they knew that they were naked; and then they sewed fig leaves together and made themselves coverings. Ok, we can stop right there."

As you close your bible, you bow your head and instruct the congregation to do likewise.

"Lord, I know that your Word is both light and life. Right now, I ask that You not only shine on, but quicken these Your people. Father, let all flesh be silent as You speak to us from the Portals of Glory. And I say now that every heart here tonight, is good ground for Your Word to grow and yield the fullest increase," is the prayer you recite after the scripture reading. You then instruct everyone to be seated again.

"Our launch scripture is a very familiar passage. It's dealing with the Fall of Mankind. Tonight, I'm going to deal with one aspect of this story in particular, and that is nakedness. Notice if you will, that Adam and his wife didn't go hide immediately. No, they chose to become the world's first fashion designers."

"Alright brother preacher!" Someone bellows from the audience.

"Make it plain!" Another urges.

"What we glean from this one verse is paramount to our relationship with the Father. God wants transparency. He wants nakedness. Turn to your neighbor and say, *Lets Get Naked*!"

The arena crackles with electricity as those three words are yelled with a fervor that surprises you.

You ride the waves of excitement and deliver a riveting sermon in which you constantly have the congregants screaming for nakedness. At the crescendo of the message, you remove your jacket to demonstrate stripping down before God.

"Getting naked is the only way that you can worship Him in spirit and in truth. And just as God was seeking Adam and Eve in Eden, He's seeking true worshippers even now! Let's get naked!" Several women begin to run back and forth across the front of the arena. After toweling your sweat away and retrieving your suit coat, you pick up your bible and begin to sing.

When was the last time you disrobed before Him?

When was the last time you let it all hang out?

When was the last time you stood naked before Him?

Transparency is what we need today.

Transparency is what we need today.

Trans-par-ency is what we need to-day!

You sing until the musicians pick it up. By the third time around, the entire arena is standing. Those who aren't weeping and speaking in tongues are singing along with gusto. You swell with pride as you look around the arena. Not only will you get a percentage on all the *Let's Get Naked* CDs and DVDs that will be sold from tonight, you've already submitted *Transparency* to *ASCAP*, so you'll be receiving royalties for your song also.

-Chapter 10-

Since *The Mountain Moving Faith Conference* your itinerary has been full. Bishop I.P. Lakes has put you on some very major events. It seems the good Bishop has taken a liking to you. You don't leave your house for less than $25,000 a sermon. Unbeknownst to you, all the top earners of the conference (those whose sermons generated the best sales) were automatically given book deals to help further their ministries. In addition, Bishop

Lakes wants to use *Transparency* for a live concert performance and recording at his *Lady Be Liberated* Conference in the fall.

The Love Movement Foundation proved to be a very profitable non-profit venture for you. Instead of personally receiving an honorarium for your speaking engagements, the foundation received a donation from whatever church benefited from your ministry.

Deacon Harper turned out to be the perfect minion to oversee the foundation also. As promised, he was able to buy a lovely home in an exclusive suburb of Detroit, as well as a Porsche Cayenne SUV.

Checking your *Patek Philippe* timepiece you make sure you're not late for your date with Jeanette. Because of her ability to give you a rise, she's earned a significant raise. You were hesitant to go any further than the occasional blowjob. But since she's proven to be discreet, you've decided to take it further. Some of your compadres in the ministry swear that secrecy is the key to any extramarital affairs they've engaged in. While there is merit to that thinking, you've noticed that if it appears you aren't trying to hide anything, you tend to get away with more. So meeting Jeanette's sexy ass on at *John Laffery's Steak on the Hearth* was a calculated risk.

After pulling up to the front entrance, you hop out of the coupe and toss your keys to the valet. The restaurant's interior is very intimate, comfortable and cozy at the same time.

"Good evening sir, how may I assist you?" the Maitre D asks.

"Reservation for Browne."

"Ok let's see, alright here we are, Browne party of two. Do you have a preference?"

"The main floor is fine, thank you," Peradventure anyone notices you, it won't look good if you're seated on the second level with Jeanette.

"Alright, follow me please."

Your table is along the far wall which is good because it will offer some privacy.

"Here you are sir; your server will be with you momentarily. Enjoy your meal."

"Thank you," you say with a slight smile, and of course you sit facing the door so there won't be any surprises.

"Good evening sir, I'm Richard and I'll be your server tonight. Would you like to see our wine list?"

"Actually I'll take a double shot of *Armadale* with three olives to start."

"I'll be right back with that for you."

Jeanette is fashionably late. And with good reason, she is looking quite divine tonight. As she approaches, you stand to greet her. The scent of *Romance by Ralph Lauren* sensuously wafts up to your nose as you pull her into your *I Wanna Fuck* embrace. That's when you hug a woman by placing your hands just atop the hump of her ass and pulling her snugly into you. Jeanette almost causes you to forget where you are.

"Damn you feel good girl."

"Thank you Pastor," she says blushing.

"Jeanette, we're not at work. Call me Lee, please," you implore.

------To Be Continued-----

Coming Soon

Lost In Eden Volume 2
-CHAPTER ONE-

Unbeknownst to you, your wife has been plotting for the past three years. She saw the handwriting on the wall as your marriage began to sour. Being the sage woman that she is, Donyetta refused to be played for a fool. As your biggest supporter, the *First Lady* wearied of always playing second fiddle to your egomaniacal desires to have the most popular church in the Motor City.

Your need to succeed at any cost blinded you to her cries for attention. Donyetta Browne is a consummate homemaker. Being a man who has to be accessible to your many sheep, you've never had to worry about how the home looked whenever someone was welcomed inside. At times you wish that she were more like you, less content to play the background, more into the business of church. This is why you *have* to engage in the extramarital dalliances that you do.

Donyetta is more of a go-getter than you think her to be, and *Rahab's Harlots* is proof of this. Knowing of your propensity to step outside of the marriage, Mrs. Browne recruited some of the most beautiful young women in the city to become mistresses of Detroit's *Religious Royalty*. This ultra-secret society of vixens blew and screws only the most prominent of pastors.

As your wife, Donyetta is privy to a lot of sensitive information, which she uses to get the right girl next to your pulpit peers. This venture has proven to be not only quite lucrative, but also extremely beneficial to all of the women.

Just as Rahab the Harlot recognized the business opportunity in hiding the enemy spies in her home, Donyetta had the foresight to recruit Jeanette to be your mistress. Your wife saw far too often how destitute and devastated the wives of many pastors were after scandalous affairs and divorces. Mrs. Browne determined that she wouldn't be one added to that list.

About The Authors

Algie Striggles

Algie was raised in Metro Detroit, Michigan. He developed a love for Literature at a young age, even winning a poetry writing contest in grade school. Algie's parents are preachers, and his work reflects many of his religious experiences. This is his first published story, so sit back and enjoy.

Anthony Striggles

Anthony, the self-proclaimed "Quiet man, with a loud Personality", is a former preacher living in Metro Detroit. A lover of the Arts, Anthony is also a Songwriter and Music Producer.

Rebecca Striggles

Rebecca was born and raised in the Metro Detroit area. The youngest of four children, reading, writing and spending time with friends and family are her passions. Rebecca is inspired by such great authors as *Toni Morrison, Eric Jerome Dickey* and *Terri Woods* just to name a few. Look for more great stories coming from this writer soon.

Arie Olah

Hailing from the Windy City, this is Arie's first offering. The native Chicagoan is a single mother of one. Look for more titles from this exciting author in the near future.

Triangle Publishing wishes to thank:

Donald Payne

David Greenway

Jonathan Stepherson.